CODE

ZERO

PAUL ORTON

"If we knew what it was we were doing, it would not be called research, would it?"

Albert Einstein

PROLOGUE

One move and it would kill him.

He knew that.

Ryan stood like a statue, staring it down.

The red eye glared back, daring him to run. But that would be suicide.

How long would he have to stand here? An hour? Two?

He breathed slowly, afraid that even the rise and fall of his chest would be enough to trigger the motion sensor.

It wouldn't be so bad if he wasn't desperate to pee. There was no way he could hold it.

He had to hope that Sparks could put their plan into action or he was in for a very uncomfortable night. If he so much as sneezed, he wouldn't live until morning.

Come on!

His stomach tightened with frustration, the tiredness already wearing away at his resolve.

The longer this went on, the worse his chances.

But there was nothing he could do except stand here, frozen to the spot.

The worst part? Even worse than having to ignore every itch and the urgent need to use the bathroom?

Deep down, he knew this was his fault.

He'd messed up.

This time, he had no-one to blame but himself.

1. KIT

Ryan stood against the wall, stifling a yawn.

Sergeant Wright glared at him. 'So, you managed to put your kit on correctly today, Jacobs?'

'Yes, sir.'

The teacher peered at Ryan's rugby shirt. 'And it looks clean. Did you remember your sock ties today?'

'Yes, sir.'

'Show me.'

Ryan lifted the top of the yellow football socks, showing the velcro ties underneath, holding them in place just below the knee.

'It's not hard, is it Jacobs?'

'No, sir.'

'So, why didn't you manage that yesterday?'

'I don't know, sir.' The truth was, he'd left the socks down on purpose. He wasn't in the mood to conform. Now he was regretting it.

He didn't understand why he had to pull the socks up; he couldn't see why it mattered. But Devonmoor Academy was not a normal school: it was strict. If you stepped out of line, you got punished. For someone like Ryan, that was bad news. Following the rules was not in his DNA. That was why he had to report to the gym stupidly early this morning. It had been a pointless act of rebellion, and he should have known better.

'Maybe spending a few weeks at home has had a detrimental effect on your discipline, Jacobs?' suggested the sergeant. 'I bet you had a lazy Christmas, didn't you?'

'Yes, sir.' There was no point denying it. The holidays had been amazing. He'd not been looking forward to starting back, but it wasn't like he had any choice.

'Well, let's remind you of the expectations we have of cadets here at the academy. And let's see if you can keep your kit looking that smart when you're running. I think three miles would be a good test, don't you?'

'Yes, sir.' Ryan sighed and glanced nervously out of the window. 'But it's pitch black out there.'

'Are you afraid of the dark, Jacobs?'

'No, sir. But I won't be able to see.'

'That's easily solved. Wait here.' Sergeant Wright disappeared into his office and emerged with a headband. On the front was a flashlight. 'Put this on.'

Ryan slipped it on, annoyed that it would mess up his hair.

'You can do the three-mile route through the grounds, around the lake. If you take longer than thirty minutes, then you'll be back here tomorrow to repeat the exercise.'

'Yes, sir.' Ryan was less than enthusiastic. That would be hard, especially given the low-light conditions and the rough terrain.

'And, Jacobs,' added Sergeant Wright with a thin smile, 'I suggest this time you keep your socks pulled up.'

'I will, sir.'

'Your time starts now.'

Ryan headed out of the gym and across the sports pitch. The headband only illuminated a few metres in front of him, but he knew the route well, having been forced to join the cross-country team by Sarah Devonmoor. Since then, he'd had to run it once a week. When you signed up for activities at the academy, you couldn't quit until the end of the school year. Another of Devonmoor's stupid rules.

The wind was freezing. Ryan tucked his hands inside the sleeves of the rugby shirt, trying to keep warm. A light drizzle soaked his clothes, making him shiver. The sooner he was back in the warm, the better. He was relieved when he reached the woods on the other side of the field. At least the trees would provide some shelter.

But in the darkness, the route didn't look that appealing. The path was muddy at the best of times. By winter, it was a bog. Ryan's trainers slipped and squelched under him. There was no point trying to avoid the puddles. He knew the course; it would only get worse. His kit would be ruined. Another thing to wash when he got back to his dorm.

The trees were packed closely together, the light from the headband casting long shadows and illuminating his breath. He tried not to think about the possibility that the batteries might run out, plunging him into total darkness. It was creepy enough as it was.

The faster he got this done, the better.

***

What the...?

He skidded to a halt as the flashlight beam illuminated something on the path ahead. It was like a scene from a horror movie. Blood. Guts.

A fox had been torn to pieces; two halves lay scattered either side of the path.

Ryan crept forwards, his heart thudding. Dead animals didn't normally bother him. As far as he was concerned, there was no point in being sentimental. Animals died all the time, especially in the wild. But something about the fox troubled him. It didn't look natural. The death looked deliberate. As if something or someone had killed the fox out of anger, or because they wanted to inflict pain.

He examined it more closely. The animal hadn't actually been ripped apart; it had been cut. There was no doubt about it: this fox had died an unnatural death.

As he stood there, Ryan heard rustling in the bushes ahead.

He shouldn't be afraid. He knew that. After all, he had a good idea what had led to the fox's demise. But it was one thing to consider facts in the cold light of day. It was another to face the unknown when you were alone in a dark forest.

He had to get out of there.

Fast.

Ryan fled, almost stumbling over his own feet in his haste to get away. He was going the wrong way, but he didn't care.

He didn't pause until he emerged from the trees and could see the school ahead. Leaning against a tree, he turned off the flashlight and took a moment to think.

How could it have happened?

What had gone wrong?

He needed to talk to Sparks. If his theory was correct, then their latest project had run amok and would cause carnage in the school grounds. They had to stop it.

But first, Ryan had to get back to the changing rooms without arousing suspicion. It was still early. With luck, most of the other cadets were still in bed and no other teachers would be about. He could creep through the corridors and out the other side of the building. That would allow him to rejoin the cross-country route, right near the end. If he timed it right, no-one would know that he'd missed the entire middle section.

One thing was for sure: the teachers mustn't know what he'd seen in the woods. If they found out what was going on, he and Sparks would be in deep trouble.

Ryan crept towards the door by the Maths block. Opening it slowly, he peeked inside. The school looked deserted. He slipped through and jogged quietly down the corridor.

'Going somewhere, Jacobs?'

The voice stopped Ryan in his tracks. He cursed inwardly as he turned to see James Sarrell standing behind him. A smart black beret marked the older cadet out as a prefect.

Ryan knew it was pointless trying to come up with an excuse, but he had to try. 'I needed the toilet.'

'Really? In the middle of a run?' Sarrell's lip curled. 'I think Sergeant Wright will be very interested to hear about this, don't you?'

2. CHEAT

'You're scum, Jacobs.' Sergeant Wright paced back and forth, his boots making a sharp clicking noise on the gym floor. 'In all my time at the academy I've never known a cadet like you. You can't even do a three-mile run without cheating.'

Ryan was back where he'd started, against the gym wall, standing to attention. Sarrell stood nearby, a smug look on his face. Watching Ryan get punished was the highlight of his week.

'I didn't cheat, sir. I just needed the toilet.'

Sergeant Wright snorted. 'Yeah, sure. And that just happened to take you on a shortcut through the school? Having trouble with your bowels, are you?'

'No, sir.'

'In which case, you are cheating scum, Jacobs. Admit it.'

Ryan clenched his jaw. He didn't speak.

'I said, ADMIT IT!' Wright was up in his face, spittle landing on Ryan's cheek.

'No, sir. It's not true.' It came out more forcefully than he intended. He could only take so much. 'It was just bad timing is all. I'll do the run again if you want.'

'If I want?' Wright laughed and looked over at Sarrell. 'If I want? Well, that's nice of you. What a magnanimous offer. I feel privileged.'

Ryan gulped. This was not going well. 'I just meant... I was trying to...'

'Quiet, Jacobs. You will not just repeat the run. You will do double the distance. Tomorrow morning. Six a.m.'

'Yes, sir.'

'And you will also admit you are cheating scum.'

Ryan glared at the sergeant. A voice inside his head screamed at him to say it, to just give in. But Ryan was not one to back down. 'No, sir.'

'You will, Jacobs. And if you keep denying it, it will only get worse. In fact, as things stand you can write it out a hundred times: "I am lazy, cheating scum and I deserve to be punished." Now, say it.'

'No, sir.'

'Now it's two hundred. I can do this all day, Jacobs. Shall we see if we can make it to a thousand? Or perhaps I should punish your roommates as well?'

'No, sir.'

Please, not that.

'Well, then, admit it. I want to hear you say it to my face.'

Ryan opened his mouth to object, but he knew it was pointless. Devonmoor Academy wasn't just strict; it belonged in the last century. He'd been brought here for trying to hack into a military network and learned the hard way what happened if you didn't follow the rules. It never ended well.

14

Reluctantly, he muttered the sentence through gritted teeth: 'I am lazy, cheating scum and I deserve to be punished.'

'That's better.' The sergeant backed off and glanced at Sarrell. 'He's hard work, this one. But we'll break him in the end. I think a six-mile run tomorrow and two hundred lines will do the trick, don't you?'

'It's a start,' agreed Sarrell. 'But there's one more thing, sir. Jacobs traipsed mud down the corridor. With your permission, I'd be happy to supervise him as he cleans it up.'

The teacher nodded. 'That seems fair. You can both miss drill this morning. Make sure he does a good job.'

'Oh, I will, sir,' said Sarrell. 'I definitely will.'

***

Ryan squeezed the mop into the bucket. Sarrell stood behind him, arms crossed.

'Enjoying the show?' asked Ryan, annoyed that Sarrell had made his punishment even worse. He was still in his sports kit, but had left his trainers at the door.

'As it happens, I am.' Sarrell raised his eyebrows. 'And I'll remind you I'm a prefect now. You refer to me as "sir".'

'Yes, *sir*,' replied Ryan, sarcasm in his voice.

'Don't make things worse, Jacobs. You're in enough trouble as it is.'

Sarrell had all the power, and he knew it. At Devonmoor, prefects had almost as much authority as the teachers. That just made Ryan feel the need to score some points of his own.

'I know why you hate me.' He blurted it out without thinking. It felt like the only way he could break through Sarrell's thick skin.

'Is that so?'

'Because of your parents.'

Sarrell hardened. His arm shot out and he grabbed hold of the mop. He forced Ryan against the wall, the mop handle against his neck. 'Keep talking, Jacobs. What about my parents?'

Ryan realised it was a mistake, but Sarrell wasn't going to back off now. 'They were spies, and they were killed because their cover was blown. All because of a hacker. You think I'm like the person who did that.'

Sarrell locked eyes with him. 'And? Your point is?'

Ryan swallowed. He wasn't sure how to answer. 'I'm not them. I shouldn't be punished for something I didn't do.'

Sarrell didn't ease up; Ryan could barely breathe.

'If it helps, Jacobs. I don't plan on punishing you for anything you *didn't* do. Only the things you did. Like making a mess of this floor.' Sarrell let go of the mop and Ryan fell to the floor, panting for breath. 'I'm assuming you got your information from Dr Torren?'

Ryan nodded, nursing his neck. He probably shouldn't say, but Sarrell had already guessed the truth.

'What the doctor doesn't realise is that I hardly knew my parents, Jacobs. They sent me from one military boarding school to another from the tender age of seven.'

Ryan had never stopped to consider what Sarrell's life was like. 'I'm sorry. I didn't...'

Sarrell kicked Ryan in the stomach, sending him sprawling. 'I don't need your sympathy. I got too much of that until I came here and the colonel helped to toughen me up. Now it's your turn. You need straightening out, Jacobs. People like you are a liability. You think you're smart, but you're selfish. You do whatever you want. You were sent here because you broke the rules and you still haven't learned your lesson. So, I'm going to teach you some discipline. And I'm going to make sure you study hard. Whenever you break a rule, I'll break you. Understand?'

Ryan looked up at Sarrell. 'Yeah, I understand.'

You're a bully and you're just looking for an excuse.

'Good. Now get mopping. You don't get breakfast until it's done. When I come back, I want to see this corridor gleam.'

'The whole corridor?'

'Yes, Jacobs. The whole corridor.'

3. PROBLEM

Ryan worked as fast as he could, but there was a lot of floor to cover. By the time Sarrell returned, he was on the last stretch.

'Well, you've been working hard. Anyone would think you were worried about missing breakfast.'

Ryan was, but not for the reason Sarrell thought. He had to talk to Sparks. He was already running late and didn't have time to mess around. He quickly finished the last corner.

'I'm done, sir.' Ryan looked hopefully at Sarrell. 'May I go?'

'Sure,' smirked Sarrell. 'But watch your back.'

Ryan knew it wasn't an empty threat, but right now Sarrell wasn't his biggest worry. He ran back to the changing rooms as fast as he could. He didn't have time to shower or change properly, so he pulled his trousers on over his sports kit and swapped his rugby shirt for his vest and academy jacket. Then he dashed to the canteen. By the time he arrived, the place was almost empty, most cadets having finished their food.

Ryan was torn. He wanted to eat, but he needed to speak to Sparks. He could see the overweight cadet sitting at the end of a long table, chatting to Kev and Ranjit.

'If you're after food, you're too late,' said one of the canteen staff, seeing him hovering in the doorway. 'You should be more punctual.'

'Sure. Sorry.'

Like it's my fault. Again.

He headed over to where Sparks was sitting and placed a hand on the boy's shoulder. 'Hey, Sparks.'

'Ryan! We were wondering what happened to you! How come you weren't at drill?'

'Sergeant Wright found a special job for me to do,' said Ryan drily. 'But forget that. We need to talk. It's urgent.'

'Always so dramatic,' said Sparks. He finished his drink and let out a loud burp. 'Oh well, if you gentlemen will excuse us.' He smiled at Kev and Ranjit, and followed Ryan out. 'What's the problem?'

'We have to check on the StealthBot. Where is it right now?'

'In engineering, where it always is. Why?'

'I think it might be on the loose.' Ryan pulled Sparks with him as he headed out of the double doors. The drizzle had turned to sleet, and Sparks didn't look too happy at being dragged outside.

'You're being ridiculous, Ryan. It can't have gone anywhere. You'll see.'

Every student at Devonmoor had their specialism, and Sparks was a genius at engineering. He'd originally designed the StealthBot for one of the robot-war competitions he often took part in. As the project grew in scale, he'd realised he had something more important than that. The StealthBot was a thing of beauty. Not only could it walk and talk, it was equipped with a whole range of sinister weapons.

But it was also stupid. It couldn't think for itself, or interpret visual data with any accuracy. It would shoot anything that moved.

Sparks realised he needed help, so he'd pressured Ryan into helping him program the robot's brain. Once it was finished, he planned to show it off to the research people at the military who already invested in some of Sparks' other inventions.

'Why not tell them about it now?' Ryan had asked, when Sparks first explained the need for secrecy.

'They take over, Ryan. It's happened before. I'm halfway through a project and then the Ministry of Defence send their experts to "help" and before you know it they're changing the blueprints, swapping bits out, turning it into something else.'

Ryan could see his point. When you create something like that, you don't want other people messing with it.

It had been a risk, of course. Devonmoor didn't like its students to have secrets, which was pretty ironic given the level of secrecy at the school. But it hadn't seemed that big a deal: after all, Sparks was always working on several inventions. Everyone knew that. Ryan couldn't imagine the teachers being too shocked if they discovered he'd been working on a robot as well. They'd get punished, of course, for using school equipment without permission, and several other minor infringements of academy rules. This was Devonmoor. But Ryan was used to that.

Now, though, if Ryan was right, the StealthBot was on the loose, and things were much more serious.

He told Sparks what he'd seen while they made their way over to the warehouse.

'It was probably just a wild animal,' said Sparks. 'There's no way the StealthBot has escaped.'

'I hope you're right.'

The engineering block was usually one of the noisiest places in the school, with the sounds of heavy machinery echoing off its walls. This early in the morning, though, it was silent.

Ryan turned to his friend. 'So, where did you put it?'

'I keep it hidden. Over in this corner.' Sparks wandered over to a messy area behind a half-finished spaceship, another of his current projects. He rummaged around, picking up a tarpaulin and moving aside a large metal sheet. He paused and turned to Ryan, concern etched into his face. 'It's not here.'

Ryan slumped onto a stool. He already knew that, but deep down he'd been hoping that he was wrong and that the corpse he'd seen earlier was just the victim of some violent predator. 'How can it have happened?'

'I don't know.' Sparks shook his head, his face pale. 'It was on standby. I left it charging overnight. It shouldn't be able to switch itself on.'

'But it did.'

'Someone might have taken it?' suggested Sparks.

'No, that doesn't explain the fox. That thing is out there. And it's looking for things to fight.'

'There must have been an error in the program,' muttered Sparks. 'You must have made a mistake.'

'*I* must have made a mistake?' exploded Ryan. 'What about the hardware? Maybe you got your wires crossed?'

'Impossible. The wiring was perfect.'

'Well, so was the program.' There was no way Ryan was taking the blame for this. 'Anyway, this was all your idea.'

'There's no point arguing.' Sparks sighed as he looked around the warehouse. 'We're in this mess, and we'll find a way out of it. We built the StealthBot, after all.'

'So, what do we do?'

'We have to get it back, Ryan. And fast. If the teachers find out, we're screwed. Both of us.'

Ryan shuddered. If he could get two hundred lines and an early morning run because he didn't pull his socks up high enough, he didn't want to think what the punishment would be for letting loose a killer robot.

'How do we find it?' he asked. 'Isn't it impossible to track? That's why it's called the StealthBot, right?'

Sparks looked up glumly. 'Yeah. We're doomed.'

'Don't worry. It can't go far. It won't be able to leave the grounds, will it?'

'Not unless it cuts its way out. It's equipped with a laser, remember. And several other weapons. It can do pretty much anything it wants.'

That wasn't an encouraging thought.

Ryan glanced at the clock. 'We have to get going. We'll look for it after lunch.'

'I guess.' Sparks was pale. 'We messed up, Ryan. Really bad.'

'Hey,' said Ryan, with a weak smile, 'welcome to my world. You get used to it after a while. It's never as bad as it seems.'

'You say that,' muttered Sparks, 'but what if they send us to Blackfell?'

Ryan didn't answer. He knew Sparks was right.

Neither of them wanted to end up there.

They had to catch the StealthBot.

Whatever it took.

4. MONEY

'Aren't we heading in the wrong direction?' Ryan called after Sparks as they hurried along the corridor. 'I thought we had quantum maths?'

'I forgot you missed drill,' said Sparks. 'There was a notice. We're not doing lessons today. We've been summoned to the Forum. You, me, and a few others.'

'The Forum?'

'This is your first one?' asked Sparks, confused.

'I only joined last term, remember?'

'It seems like longer.'

'You're telling me,' agreed Ryan. It felt like he'd been at Devonmoor for years. 'So, what do we do in the Forum?'

'That's where the action happens. The Project. You know, old Lord Devonmoor's crazy plan to solve world problems using our skills and cunning?'

Ryan had been told about The Project when he first came to the school, but he'd never seen it in action. 'How does it work?'

'You'll see.' Sparks huffed and puffed as they made their way up several flights of stairs. 'Ready?'

'I guess.'

Sparks pushed open the double doors, and Ryan took a sharp breath as they walked into the vast room beyond. It seemed the academy still held some surprises.

The room was a perfect circle. Windows swept around the edge, perfectly joined so the ceiling appeared to be floating in the air. They were right at the top of the academy, and Ryan could see the grounds below, stretching into the distance. It was an impressive view. Even with grey skies, daylight filled the room.

There were several circular tables and stools. Some had computers while others were bare. At the centre of the room was a large space, dominated by an interactive whiteboard. Mrs Tracey was standing by it, looking impatient. Next to her stood a man in a suit that Ryan didn't recognise.

Several students had arrived and were dragging stools over to form a semi-circle in the middle. Ryan copied Sparks as he picked one up and placed it in formation with the others. Once he sat down, he checked out which other cadets had been selected.

Lee was there, and Jael, and so was Ranjit. But there was no sign of Kev or Ayana, and there were a few cadets that Ryan didn't know.

As he looked around, Sarah Devonmoor caught his eye.

'Why are you here, Jacobs?'

'Dunno,' he admitted.

'You realise that in the Forum we have to work as a team?'

Ryan shrugged, and she didn't push the point any further.

She would have to be here, wouldn't she?

He and Sarah had never got on well. He had no idea what he'd done to annoy her, but she hated his guts.

Still, it was better than Sarrell. As groups went, it looked promising. It could be much, much worse.

'I think we're all here,' said Mrs Tracey, scanning her list. 'Let's make a start. As you are no doubt aware, we call a Forum when there is an issue that we need your help with. We select the cadets we feel are best-equipped to contribute to the problem at hand. The fact that you are sitting here means that together you will have the right skill-sets to offer unique insights and solutions. You will not attend lessons until you solve the problem or the Forum is dissolved. We expect you to focus all of your time and energy on this issue. Does everyone understand?'

The cadets nodded. Ryan felt his stomach tense. Right now, it was going to be hard to focus on anything other than the killer robot.

'I'd like to introduce you to Mr Harding,' said Mrs Tracey. 'He is from the Serious Financial Crimes department of Scotland Yard and wishes to discuss some significant problems they are facing at present.'

'Good morning, children,' said Mr Harding.

It wasn't a good start. The students visibly tensed at his words. Mr Harding hadn't made himself any friends, that was for sure, but he carried on regardless.

'I'm surprised I've been asked to speak to you about this today, as I'm sure that the problem we're dealing with is way over your heads. But the government asked me to come here, and I've had to sign the Official Secrets Act, so I'm willing to give it a go.' He sighed and looked at them. 'Where do I begin? Money is transferred between bank accounts all the time. Every day, every hour, every minute, every second. Thousands, millions, billions of pounds. Some of it gets transferred from one country to another.'

'Yes,' said Mrs Tracey, impatiently, 'the cadets study this in Global Economics. Do go on.'

Ryan fidgeted in his seat. The stools had no backs, and it was hard to relax when you had to hold your body upright. That was probably deliberate, to make the cadets concentrate.

'Recently, several very rich and significant individuals have had money stolen from their accounts,' continued Mr Harding. 'Some have lost millions.'

'But surely you can just trace the transactions?' blurted out one of the younger cadets. 'It's all recorded, after all.'

Mr Harding looked annoyed. 'Yes, surprisingly, we thought of that. Even us thickies at Scotland Yard thought that would be a good idea. But whoever is doing this is very clever. They don't make single lump sum transactions. They break it down into much, much smaller amounts. These are then paid to thousands of other bank accounts. Then, the same

27

thing happens from those accounts. We end up chasing tiny amounts of money, and we don't have the resources to do it. We can't work out how the thief eventually gets hold of the money. Or how they access so many accounts. Our best people have been working on this for days, and they can't crack it. So, we're hoping you can.'

'Thank you, Mr Harding,' said Mrs Tracey. 'We're going to split into small groups and agree on the key questions we should be asking. You don't need to come up with any answers at this point, just questions. What do we need to know? You have fifteen minutes.'

5. QUESTIONS

Ryan found himself at a table with Sarah and Jael. It wasn't a great team, but he only had to put up with them for a fifteen-minute brainstorming session. How hard could it be?

'It doesn't make sense,' said Sarah. 'Either someone must have thousands of bank accounts, or they have access to that number of real ones. But how could anyone carry out a hack on that kind of scale?'

She looked at Ryan, as if expecting some sort of answer.

'I don't know,' he admitted. 'It's not easy to hack into banks. There are multiple checks and passwords. Even to get access to a few accounts would take hours.'

'Even for an expert?' asked Jael.

'Yeah. It's hard work. Banks have the best cyber-security and firewalls. They're tough targets.'

Sarah frowned. 'We need to know if they're making loads of fake bank accounts or whether they're using accounts that belong to real people.'

Jael had a sudden thought. 'Maybe loads of people are in on it. It could be a big conspiracy.

Thousands of people all working together to transfer the money between them and lose it in the system.'

'Possibly,' allowed Sarah. 'But they'd still need to hack into the rich people's accounts to make the initial transfers.'

'Unless it's insurance fraud,' pointed out Jael. 'Maybe the rich guys are in on it too. They always get their money back somehow. Rich people are like that.'

They carried on for a few minutes, bouncing ideas off each other, but Ryan couldn't focus. He looked out of the window, at the beautiful grounds below. In the distance he could see the Devonmoor lake. Somewhere in the trees behind, he caught a flash of red. He watched intently, wondering if it was the StealthBot or one of the soldiers that patrolled the grounds.

There it was again. Another flash, like a laser sight being pointed right at him. He shuddered.

'Are we boring you, Jacobs?' Sarah snapped him out of his reverie.

'No, sorry. Just thinking hard. You know, about the problem.'

'Want to share any of those profound thoughts with us?'

Ryan tried to come up with something on the spot, but he couldn't think. 'I, er, wondered if Jael's right, about this being a big scam involving thousands of people. Well, there would be some way they'd communicate. Someone must be co-ordinating it, right? Maybe we could find out how they're doing that?'

Sarah didn't look impressed. 'Brilliant, as usual.'

She didn't have time to lay into him any more, as the groups were called back together.

As they dragged their stools back to the centre, Ryan grabbed Sparks by the shoulder. 'I think I just saw it,' he hissed, 'out by the lake.'

Sparks nodded. 'Keep an eye on it. Hopefully, it'll stay there. Then we'll be able to find it at lunch.'

'There's one more thing,' added Ryan. 'It was pointing its laser at me.'

'But it can't...'

'Settle down, cadets,' ordered Mrs Tracey. Everyone else was already seated, and they couldn't say any more without being overheard. 'What questions did you come up with? Where does our investigation begin?'

'Are these all real bank accounts?' said Jael. 'I mean, do they belong to actual people? Or are they decoys?'

'They're all real,' said Mr Harding. 'We located the people who owned the accounts the money moved through, and interviewed everyone. It took days. There were ninety-year-old widows and middle-aged parents, students and mechanics, factory workers and cleaners. They knew nothing about it. They didn't know their accounts had been used to transfer money until they saw their bank statements.'

'But there must have been a pattern,' pressed on Jael. 'They must have had something in common.'

'Yeah, is there any possibility of a conspiracy?' added Ranjit. 'Could all these people be working together?'

'We've ruled it out.' Mr Harding was emphatic. 'The people who lost money in the first place are all well-connected, but not the others. They live all over the country. They have different backgrounds. And they have nothing to gain. The money came in. Then it went out, in even smaller chunks, to even more people. Then the same again.'

'Someone got to keep it,' pointed out Sarah. 'Couldn't you trace it until it stopped?'

'We did to a point.' Mr Harding wiped his forehead with a handkerchief. 'Sometimes, small amounts of money just stayed in someone's account, or some part of it did. One woman was left with a hundred pounds. Another man was fifty pounds better off. We assumed these people might know something, as they profited from the scam. But after intense questioning, we concluded otherwise.'

'Can *we* question them?' asked Ranjit, raising his eyebrows. It wasn't a stupid question, given his skill at reading people, but Mr Harding didn't know that.

'No, you can't,' he said, sharply. 'I think they might be suspicious if we let a twelve-year-old interrogate them, don't you?'

Ranjit narrowed his eyes. 'Just for the record, I'm thirteen.'

Mrs Tracey stood up before things got any more heated. 'Does anyone have any more questions?'

6. YELLOW

The morning dragged as the students in the Forum continued to discuss the thefts.

As soon as the siren went to announce the start of the lunch period, Ryan and Sparks raced down to the canteen.

'We'll eat fast,' said Sparks, 'so we have enough time.'

'Sure,' agreed Ryan. 'As long as I get some food. I skipped breakfast, remember?'

They were among the first to the computer terminals by the serving area. At Devonmoor, you had to answer questions before you got breakfast or lunch. Your score determined the quality of your meal.

Ryan's first question was about astronomy, but he hadn't been paying attention during the lesson they'd had last week: 'Which of the following is NOT one of Uranus' moons? A. Titania, B. Kordia, C. Oberon, D. Ariel, E. Umbriel.'

Ryan hesitated, then chose 'D', but it wasn't right. A red cross appeared on the screen.

'Come on, Ryan,' he muttered to himself. His stomach was rumbling.

The next question was about biology: 'How many ribs are there in a human rib cage? A. 16, B, 18, C. 22, D. 24, E. 26.'

This one he knew; he could remember Mr Cho teaching them about it. He selected 'D' and saw the green tick he was hoping for.

The third question was even easier, especially for Ryan. 'Which of the following is NOT a primary component of firewall architecture: A. Binary Splitting, B. Advanced Authentication, C. Packet Filtering, D. Application Gateways.' He selected 'A' and got another green tick.

Which was good, because the next two questions were a total bust. His final score was only two out of five, and he slouched towards the serving area.

'What's on the menu for a purple,' he asked, holding up his ticket. 'Let me guess: dog food?'

The woman behind the counter gave a sour smile. 'Nope. That would at least have meat in it.'

She grabbed a bowl and slopped in some grey-brown watery stew, before placing it on his tray.

'That's what you get for a purple?' asked Ryan, disappointed. 'What would you get for a red?'

'The same.' The woman shrugged. 'But without this.' She handed him some bread.

'Thanks. I guess.'

Ryan knew better than to argue. He already had a reputation. If you mouthed off at the canteen staff, you lost the opportunity to eat. It wasn't worth it.

He glanced up and saw Sparks settling down at their usual table at the other side of the room. He headed over, wondering how they would catch the StealthBot when they found it. Because of that, he wasn't paying attention. If he had been, he might have noticed Sarrell.

As Ryan went to step forward, Sarrell hooked his foot and tripped him up. He crashed to the floor, his stew splattering over the canteen floor. He rolled on his side to see Sarrell standing over him.

'Making a mess of the floor again, Jacobs?' sneered the bully. 'I would have thought you'd learned your lesson this morning.'

Ryan swore and tried to kick Sarrell hard in the balls. He should have known better. There was no point fighting: Sarrell had been trained in martial arts and was the toughest kid at the academy. He was older, bigger and stronger than Ryan.

Sarrell grabbed his foot and lifted Ryan up by the legs, holding him upside down. 'Why don't I give you a hand clearing that up? You don't mind if I use you as a mop, do you?'

'No, don't...' Ryan had barely started to speak before Sarrell dragged him one way then the other, using Ryan's hair to smear the stew around the floor. Ryan tried to use his arms to push his head away, but he wasn't strong enough, and Sarrell swept them away with his feet.

'WHAT is going on here?' Ryan twisted his head to see Colonel Keller standing nearby, hands on hips.

'Cadet Jacobs had a little accident,' said Sarrell. 'I was just teaching him to be more careful in the future.'

Ryan was still hanging upside down, gripped by his ankles. Even now, Sarrell didn't let go.

Colonel Keller's next question was so unexpected, it caught Ryan off guard. 'Cadet Jacobs, can you explain to me why you are wearing *yellow* socks?'

Ryan glanced up and groaned. Sarrell's little stunt meant his trouser legs had fallen some way up his leg, revealing his sports kit underneath. 'I didn't have time to get changed, sir.'

'You didn't have time to get changed.' Colonel Keller emphasised every word, and Ryan knew he was in trouble.

Sarrell let go, dropping Ryan to the floor, leaving him to scramble around in the mess.

Ryan clambered to his feet, his face red. It was just like the colonel to overlook the big issues and focus on the small ones, especially when it suited him. "Aren't you going to have a go at Sarrell? For bullying me? You saw what he was doing!'

'Don't try to change the subject, Jacobs. Did Sarrell get you dressed this morning?'

'No, but...'

'Then stop trying to blame him for your mistakes. Follow me. Right now.'

Ryan glanced over at Sparks. His friend looked worried. Their plan to catch the StealthBot was in jeopardy. Ryan mouthed an apology as he left. He had no idea what the colonel would do, but it wouldn't be good.

This was turning into a really bad day.

7. DIRTY

'It's like he wants to be punished.'

Ryan stood to attention in the empty gym. Colonel Keller and Sergeant Wright were right in front of him, deciding his fate.

'I've already given him two hundred lines, and he has to do a six-mile run tomorrow morning.' Sergeant Wright sighed with disbelief. 'What more can I do?'

'Perhaps he likes to be dirty?' suggested the colonel, an edge to his voice. 'Is that it, Jacobs?'

'No, sir.' Ryan hated it. They'd made him change back into his filthy sports kit. The rugby shirt was damp and stunk of sweat and the socks and shorts were splattered with stagnant mud. The worst part was that he still had stew in his hair.

'Have you ever seen anything like it?' Sergeant Wright shook his head. He took it as a personal affront if any of the cadets weren't smart.

'Actually, I have,' mused the colonel. 'Just once. The Outlier had a similar attitude.'

It was rare for any teacher to mention the Outlier, a former student of Devonmoor Academy who was now one of its greatest enemies. Ryan almost asked about him, but he'd only get into more trouble if he spoke.

'What do you suggest?' asked Sergeant Wright. 'An early morning run every day this week?' That was typical. Long runs were his answer to everything.

The colonel was a lot more creative. 'Agreed. Including Saturday and Sunday. But, then again, don't you think that's going to be too difficult for him? You know how Jacobs hates getting changed.'

'What do you mean?' asked Sergeant Wright, perplexed.

'We can't expect him to keep putting on his sports kit, then changing into his academy uniform. All that changing and showering is too much like hard work, isn't that right, Jacobs?'

Ryan wasn't sure what to say. 'Yes, sir,' he offered, hoping he'd made the right choice.

'You see? I think we need to go easy on the rules for a boy like him. So, we'll make a special exception. Jacobs doesn't need to get changed. He can stay in that kit. *All* the time. No showering and no changing. Perhaps he will learn to appreciate the value of good hygiene by going without.'

Sergeant Wright's lip curled. 'How long are you thinking?'

'A normal kid would break in three days, but this is Jacobs. I think we'll make it a week. You'd like that wouldn't you, Jacobs?'

'No, sir.'

Surely, the colonel wasn't serious?

'Well, you should have thought about that before you opted to wear your sports kit under your uniform. This way you might think twice about wearing the correct clothes. Outside you can wear your trainers. Inside, you don't get shoes.'

The full horror of what the colonel was proposing began to sink in. 'Permission to ask a question, sir?' he said. He didn't want to risk annoying the man any further.

'Ask away, Jacobs.' The colonel grinned. He was enjoying watching Ryan squirm.

'Can I take it off at night?'

'Oh no. That would mean all the effort of putting it back on again in the morning. You sleep in it. I may get one of the prefects to check on you.'

We all know who that will be, thought Ryan. *Sarrell*.

The kit was damp and disgusting. He wasn't sure he'd be able to bear it.

'You'll see, Sergeant. After three or four days wearing the same kit day after day, he'll come crawling in here, begging you to let him shower and change.'

'Probably.'

'And you know what you need to do if he does?' The colonel looked over at his colleague, a wicked gleam in his eye.

'What?'

'You say "no", Sergeant. And you enjoy the look on his desperate little face. He needs to remember this for years to come. Every single time he pulls on his uniform, he needs to think about the consequences of not wearing it correctly. After this week, he'll be the best-dressed cadet at this academy.'

'I doubt that,' said Sergeant Wright, 'but if you're right, it will be the most impressive turnaround I've ever seen.'

***

Ryan raced over to the engineering block. He'd missed any chance of lunch and it was the most likely place he'd find Sparks.

Sure enough, there he was, in the corner by the spaceship. His eyes lit up when he saw Ryan. 'You made it!'

'Just. How long do we have?'

'About half an hour. But are you meant to be doing a run?'

'No.' Ryan glanced down at his muddy kit. 'This is just what I have to wear for the next week thanks to Colonel Keller.'

'A whole week? In that? You're gonna stink.'

'You think I don't know that?'

'That's harsh. Even for the colonel.' There was a note of awe in Sparks voice.

Ryan was irritated. 'Can we just get on with this?'

'Sure. I brought something that might cheer you up.' Sparks pulled up a trouser leg and removed a crusty bread roll from his grey sock. 'I retrieved this off the floor before it got cleaned up, in case you're hungry.'

Ryan stared at it. He was starving. He'd missed breakfast and lunch. This was his only opportunity to eat before dinner. By then he'd have gone twenty-four hours without food. But the roll had been on the floor and then in a sock. Was he that desperate?

'Do not tell anyone about this. Ever.' He took the roll and crammed it in his mouth. He tried to ask his next question with his mouth full. 'If we find the StealthBot, how do we capture it?'

'We use this.' Sparks pulled an impressive looking device out from behind a storage locker. It looked like a ray-gun from an old science-fiction movie. 'It's an EMP blaster. It should temporarily disable anything electrical within five metres.'

'That's pretty close.' Ryan had been hoping they'd be able to capture the StealthBot from a distance.

'It has to be, for the pulse to be effective. Anyway, I thought you programmed it not to fire at humans. We should be safe, shouldn't we?'

'Sure. It can't hurt us.'

But then, it can't turn itself on and disappear in the middle of the night, either.

Ryan didn't want to scare Sparks, but he was no longer sure what the StealthBot was capable of.

Sparks was oblivious to the danger. 'Then what are we waiting for? Let's go.'

8. HUNT

'You say you saw it around here?' Sparks looked comical, wandering through the woods with the blaster. If the situation wasn't so serious, Ryan would have smiled.

'Yeah. I thought it was aiming its laser at me.'

'Well, at least it didn't fire.'

Not yet, anyway.

They were standing at the lakeshore, surrounded by undergrowth. Ryan walked over to a muddy patch of ground. 'I think it's been here. Look.' Part of a three-pronged footprint was visible, like an alien had stamped on the ground.

'That's the StealthBot alright.' Sparks looked around. 'You're sure it's safe?'

'Will you stop asking that?' Ryan ran his hand through his hair, then wrinkled up his nose in disgust as he felt congealed stew on his fingers. 'It should be.'

Sparks gripped the blaster tightly. 'Looks like it headed this way.'

They crept forward, away from the lake and through the bushes.

'Have you worked out what went wrong yet?' asked Sparks. 'Do you know how we fix it?'

'No,' shot back Ryan. 'Do you?'

Sparks shook his head. 'For now, we just need to unplug it's central processor to make it safe. Make sure this doesn't happen again.'

'You think?' Ryan couldn't help being sarcastic. He liked Sparks, but the kid had a habit of stating the obvious.

Ryan froze as he heard something up ahead. He held up his hand. Sparks stood still, but he breathed heavily in Ryan's ear.

'Shh,' urged Ryan.

They listened intently.

There it was again.

Ryan glanced around. There was a large bush to the left. He pointed towards it and Sparks nodded. They crept over and slipped behind it.

It wasn't the robot. It was one of the soldiers that patrolled Devonmoor's grounds. Ryan had found it weird at first, having them guarding the school. But Devonmoor was a school with secrets, and those secrets needed protecting.

The soldier wouldn't shoot them. But he probably would send them back. He looked like he meant business. He was holding a gun, checking out the area. He lowered his weapon and took out a walkie-talkie.

'This is Cobra One Seven. False alarm. I thought I heard something, but it must have been the wind. No sign of any intruder here.'

Ryan glanced over at Sparks. The boy had gone white and looked like he was struggling to breathe.

43

He wasn't used to this level of danger. Ryan put his hand on Sparks shoulder.

The soldier carried on moving. A few minutes later, he was out of sight.

'That was close,' gasped Sparks.

'Too close,' agreed Ryan. 'Looks like we're not the only ones out hunting this afternoon.'

'Let's hope we find it first.'

Ryan wasn't sure whether Sparks was more worried about his precious StealthBot being destroyed, or whether he'd just rather avoid having to give a very awkward explanation to the teachers about how it got there in the first place.

With any luck, they would find the robot before the soldiers did, disable it with the EMP and get it back to the engineering block. Was that too much to ask?

'You sure this is the right direction?' asked Ryan. 'I haven't seen any more footprints.'

'It can't have disappeared. The one we found definitely showed it moving in this direction.'

'So where is it?'

Sparks shrugged. 'We only have another fifteen minutes. We're running out of time.'

'Then let's move.' Ryan started jogging forward, throwing caution to the wind.

The ground was muddier here, a large puddle dominating the middle of a small clearing.

'Sparks, look at this.' Ryan crouched down to examine some marks, inches from the muddy puddle. As he glanced up, he saw Sparks frozen in place, the EMP gun pointing at the ground. 'What's wrong?'

He followed Spark's gaze, twisting around to look behind him.

There it was.

Eight feet tall.

Black shiny plating covering its massive body.

Staring at them with its single red eye.

Its weapons aimed at them.

The StealthBot.

9. THREAT

Something whirred and clicked.

One gun pointed at Ryan, another at Sparks.

Sparks was trembling, the gun hanging at his side, useless.

'THREAT DETECTED.' The metallic voice made Ryan's blood freeze.

'Shoot it,' hissed Ryan.

But Sparks wouldn't budge. They all stood there looking at each other. Sparks at the robot. The robot at Ryan. Ryan at Sparks.

'Fine, I'll do it.' Ryan jumped forward and grabbed the EMP blaster from Sparks. He turned towards the StealthBot, his finger on the trigger, ready to fire.

But as he lifted the gun, red light flashed from the robot's own weapon straight at the blaster.

It felt red hot in Ryan's hands. He cried out in pain and let go. The remains fell to the floor, a pile of molten metal and smoking ash.

'THREAT NEUTRALISED.'

'W-W-What do we do now?' whimpered Sparks, backing away.

Ryan sucked his hand, which felt hot and sore. 'We get out of here! RUN!'

As they turned and bolted, there was a clicking noise, and seconds later the StealthBot opened fire, silent bullets ripping into the surrounding trees, kicking up the mud.

'Keep moving,' yelled Ryan.

Sparks didn't need to be told. For once, he was running faster than Ryan, scared for his life.

A few minutes later, they stumbled into a clearing, panting, Sparks doubled over in pain.

'Did you get hit?' asked Ryan, concerned.

'No... just... exhausted...' Sparks couldn't say any more.

'I think we lost it. I don't think it gave chase.'

Sparks nodded.

'We better keep moving. We have to get back. It must be time for the afternoon session of the Forum.' Ryan stepped forward, but almost tripped as his foot caught on a wire. 'What the-'

He looked up at Sparks, realising what was about to happen. 'Don't say anything, ok? I'll handle this.'

Sparks looked bewildered, but nodded. He had no idea what Ryan was talking about.

A few seconds later, he found out.

Soldiers stormed into the clearing, weapons raised.

'GET DOWN ON THE FLOOR! NOW!' Ryan dropped to his knees and then on to his front. Sparks copied him.

'It's just some cadets, sir.' One soldier walked over and nudged Ryan with his foot. 'What are you doing out here, boy?'

'Cross-country. What do you think?' Ryan hoped that wearing the kit would work in his favour.

'How come your mate isn't dressed for it?' The soldier thumbed in Sparks' direction.

'He's just here to make sure I don't cheat.'

It was a weak excuse, but the soldiers didn't care. They were here to find an intruder, not deal with unruly cadets. 'You and your mate need to get back to the school, double-quick. The woods are out of bounds.'

'Sure. Why?'

'We think there's an intruder. He's killed one of the dogs. So, you get to safety, you hear me? And don't come back.'

'Yes, sir.' Ryan climbed up and helped Sparks to his feet. They hurried off towards the school.

'You ok?' Ryan asked as soon as they were some distance away.

Sparks looked like he was going to be sick. 'Never a dull moment with you around, is there?' he replied.

Ryan grinned. 'Nope.'

'I don't know why you're so happy,' moaned Sparks. 'We failed, Ryan. We didn't get the StealthBot.'

'True.' Ryan shrugged. 'But we're alive, aren't we? And for the moment, I'm grateful for that.'

***

Ryan kicked off his trainers as they entered the building. Sparks was keen to get straight back to the Forum.

'You go ahead,' said Ryan. 'I need the toilet.'

It wasn't strictly true, but he couldn't spend a moment longer without cleaning the stew from his hair.

Rushing into the boys' washroom, he ran water into the sink. He didn't notice the cubicle door open behind him.

'It must be my lucky day,' said Sarrell, a wicked grin on his face.

Not surprisingly, Ryan didn't feel the same way. 'You've had your fun. Leave me alone.'

'Did you have to do another run?' Sarrell walked next to Ryan and looked at him in the mirror.

'Not yet,' replied Ryan. 'But you'll be pleased to know I have to do six miles every morning before drill. And I have to wear this kit all week. I don't even get to shower. Happy?'

Sarrell gave a thin smile. 'You have to give the colonel credit. He knows how to inflict pain.'

Ryan glared at him. 'So do you.'

Sarrell grabbed him by his hair. 'That's true, Jacobs. And I don't remember giving you permission to clean your hair. But if you're so desperate to do it, maybe I can help.' He dragged Ryan over to the cubicles.

'You're gonna stick my head down a toilet? Really?' Ryan's voice quavered. 'Isn't that a little lacking in originality, even for you, Sarrell?'

'Actually, I'm giving you a choice. Either I do it to you, or you do it yourself. But if you do it, you get to choose the toilet. What's it to be?'

Ryan hesitated, trying to think of a way out.

'If you don't answer in three seconds, then I decide for you.'

'Fine. I'll do it.'

Like heck, I will.

Sarrell let go of Ryan's hair and pushed him forward. 'Go on then. Stick your head right in. If your hair isn't dripping, then we'll go again.'

Ryan pretended to check out the three cubicles, stalling for time. He was hoping someone else might walk in and provide a distraction.

'Hurry up.' Sarrell narrowed his eyes.

Ryan turned and bolted. It wasn't the best plan, but he was out of options.

Unfortunately, Sarrell didn't even let him make it to the door. He grabbed hold of Ryan and kneed him in the stomach, before dragging him back over to a cubicle.

Ryan barely caught his breath before Sarrell grabbed his hair and pushed his face into the toilet, the strong smell of urine filling his nostrils.

'No, please...'

Sarrell smirked and pulled the handle.

A torrent of water erupted around Ryan's head, coursing up his nose and drenching his hair. As soon as it finished, Sarrell let go and Ryan pulled his head up, coughing and spluttering.

Water dripped from his hair onto his rugby shirt as he lay sprawled on the bathroom floor.

Sarrell stood watching him, shaking his head in mock sympathy. 'Sometimes I almost feel sorry for you, Jacobs. But like I said earlier, someone's got to toughen you up. After all, what are you Jacobs?'

'Huh?'

Sarrell kicked him hard in the leg and Ryan cried out in pain. 'What did Sergeant Wright call you? What do you have to write for your lines?'

Ryan wiped water off his nose with his sleeve. 'I'm lazy, cheating scum and I deserve to be punished.'

'I didn't hear you.'

'I'm lazy, cheating scum and I deserve to be punished.'

'Ain't that the truth. You'll thank me in the end. By the time I'm finished with you, you'll bogwash yourself, just for the fun of it. Think about that.'

With that, Sarrell walked off, whistling, leaving Ryan on the floor.

10. REVELATION

Ryan made it to the session just in time. Mrs Tracey wasn't someone who tolerated you showing up late. He'd found that out the hard way.

He got some strange looks as he scuffed his way into the room in his dirty sports kit, his hair dripping wet.

'I'm assuming there is some reason for your current appearance?' enquired Mrs Tracey, bemused.

'Yes, ma'am. Colonel Keller is punishing me. I have to stay like this all week.'

'Why's that?'

Ryan shrugged, as if he didn't care. 'Isn't it obvious? I'm lazy, cheating scum, ma'am.'

Some cadets laughed.

'Well, let's press on.' Mrs Tracey glanced around at the gathered students. There was no sign of Mr Harding. He'd probably gone back to Scotland Yard. 'This morning we did a lot of information gathering. As you'll recall, vast sums of money are being stolen from very rich and significant people. The money then moves through genuine accounts, all the time being broken down into smaller and smaller amounts.

Despite their best efforts, the Serious Financial Crimes Squad cannot work out how the thieves are doing it, or how the money makes its way to them using this method. Besides that, Scotland Yard are persuaded that this is not some giant conspiracy between all the account holders.'

'We can't rule it out though,' pointed out Ranjit.

'No. But we can make a working assumption.' Mrs Tracey took a breath. 'We then explored the probability of any individual being able to hack that number of accounts. It hardly seems possible, but,' she glanced at Ranjit, 'we can't rule that out either.'

'So, what do we do now?' asked one of the younger cadets. Ryan could tell that Mrs Tracey was irritated by the question, but he admired the kid for speaking up.

'This afternoon we focus on numbers and patterns.' Mrs Tracey walked over to the desk and picked out an enormous pile of papers. 'This is a list of the sort codes and account numbers that the perpetrator has used, in chronological order, along with the amounts transferred. Some of them were accessed only a matter of seconds apart. Marquez, Young, Zivai, you get to examine these numbers. You're looking for patterns, repeating sets, anything that might give us a clue why these specific accounts were chosen.'

Lee, Jael and a younger cadet took their place at a table and leafed through the pages.

'Jacobs, Sparks, Devonmoor, Yu; you will also try to identify patterns and connections. But you'll be doing it using computers. The data has been preloaded onto the machines. Use analysis software, or a program of your own. But find me a pattern.'

Ryan headed to a table with screens, followed by Sarah Devonmoor, Kelvin Sparks and Shilin Yu, a kid who Ryan often saw in the computer lab.

'The rest of you will split into two teams and examine the lifestyles, personalities and family situations of the account holders. We're looking for anything at all that links them, that might help us know why they were selected to be a part of this scam.' Mrs Tracey deposited two huge piles of papers on each of the desks.

'What happened to saving the rainforests?' muttered the small cadet.

Mrs Tracey gave him a sharp look. 'Does everyone understand their tasks?'

The cadets nodded, but now that they faced stacks of complex data, they looked less than keen.

'Good. Then begin.'

A low murmur broke out across the room as the teams got themselves organised.

'At least we get computers,' said Sarah.

'Too right,' agreed Ryan. He was glad they didn't expect him to work through the printed information like the other groups. But something was bugging him: why was Sarah in the techie group? It made sense that Sparks would be there, given his knowledge of hardware, and Yu was one of the most gifted programmers in the academy. But Sarah?

'How come you're on this team?' he blurted out.

'Typical. You don't think I should be here, just because I'm a girl.'

'It's not that,' said Ryan, flustered. 'It's just we're all specialists and you're not.'

'Really? So, what is my specialism, Jacobs?' Sarah glared at him across the table.

Ryan opened his mouth, then closed it again, trying to remember.

'Come on, spit it out.'

'It's, it's...' As he fumbled for words, Ryan realised he didn't know. He just knew her as Lady Devonmoor's granddaughter. She was a strict prefect and always acted like the perfect cadet. 'Leadership?'

'Too vague. Guess again.'

'I-I-I have no idea,' admitted Ryan.

'It's computing. Before you came to this school, I was Mr Davids' top student.'

'You're a hacker?' Ryan stared at her, his mouth hanging open.

Sarah gave him a look of disgust. 'No, I'm a cyber-security specialist. Hackers are, as I think we've established, lazy, cheating scum.'

Ryan ignored the dig. He'd never imagined she was any good with computers. No-one had ever mentioned it before. 'So, how come you're never in the computing labs?'

'I have a computer in my room,' she replied. 'Not all of us need to spend all our time sucking up to Mr Davids. Besides, I can't stand the smell in there, especially if you're around.'

Ryan didn't respond. His head was spinning. It all made sense now: this was why Sarah hated him. He'd taken her place as the best computing student at the academy and she was jealous.

Shilin cleared his throat, keen to get going with the task. 'So, how do you want to do this? Do we all work together or what?'

Sarah tutted and looked away. 'How's that gonna work? We're programmers. We can't exactly share a keyboard.'

'Let's take a computer each,' agreed Ryan, relieved. He always worked better alone.

Sarah started giving orders: 'Yu, you analyse the account numbers. Sparks, you're on hardware: look at the device identification numbers and see if these people are logging in using a particular brand of phone or laptop. Maybe the circuit board has a flaw. I'll correlate IP addresses against physical locations, and do some digital mapping. Jacobs, you can...' She trailed off, all the important jobs already assigned.

'... go jump in the lake?' suggested Ryan.

'It looks like you already did,' shot back Sarah, looking at his soaking-wet hair. 'Why don't you just do whatever you want. You always do, anyway. But I expect you to find something decent from all these numbers.'

'Sure.'

He suppressed a smile as he settled in front of a keyboard and got to work.

This was what he needed: some time alone to work on the problem.

But it wasn't the bank transfers he was interested in.

It was what had gone wrong with the robot.

11. TARGET

Ryan huddled over his machine, scanning the code, oblivious to the others in the Forum.

When Sparks had first asked him to help with the StealthBot, he'd known it would be a lot of work, but he owed Sparks, so he'd agreed. Besides, a part of him relished the challenge. He'd always been interested in Artificial Intelligence and it wasn't every day you had the opportunity to program a robot's brain. And if nothing else, it was another way to break some rules and get one over on the teachers.

Now, though, things were out of control. If someone got hurt, or killed, then Ryan and Sparks would get much more than a detention. They would be sent to Blackfell, the boot camp from hell for young people who posed a serious risk to national security. Ryan shuddered. He had to work out what had gone wrong. Why had the StealthBot gone crazy? How had it broken its programming?

He pulled up the key subroutine: the Asimov protocol. This was where he was most likely to find the problem. It wasn't easy to focus with the noise of the Forum, but he did his best to shut it out as he analysed the code.

It was all there. Everything as it should be. The robot should in no circumstances be able to harm a human being, or allow them to be harmed. Asimov's first law of robotics. He hadn't missed it out; he hadn't made a mistake.

But had the robot broken the rule?

The fox wasn't human. There was nothing in the code that would stop the robot from ripping it to pieces. The same was true for the unfortunate Alsatian that had come across it in the woods.

But it shot at us.

Had it? Or had they been warning shots? After all, neither he nor Sparks had been hit, even though the threat had felt very real. Still, he'd almost burned his hand when the robot had shot the EMP blaster. Even that seemed to breach the Asimov protocol.

Perhaps the robot couldn't tell the difference. Maybe it didn't know they were human. If it thought he and Sparks were animals, then that wouldn't stop it from shooting them. But they'd done extensive testing on this. The robot was more than capable of discerning a person from a beast. It had five different methods, from mapping the heat signature to visual recognition systems. All of them couldn't malfunction at the same time.

He glanced out of the window. The Devonmoor lake looked grey and gloomy under the cloudy sky. There it was again. A flash of red.

Was the robot watching him? Was it aiming at him?

'What's that, Jacobs?' Sarah Devonmoor was standing at his shoulder. She leaned forward, reading the code.

'Nothing,' he said. He hadn't heard her approach. 'I mean, it's just the start of some analysis software I'm designing, to work through the bank account data.'

'Really?' She didn't look convinced.

Ryan fidgeted on the stool, wanting to close down the screen, but knowing that would look even more suspicious. He fiddled with the buttons on his rugby shirt, feeling very hot. He hoped Sarah wasn't as good at computing as she said.

'This isn't anything to do with data analysis, Jacobs.' She reached forward and scrolled through the code. 'And there's no way you've done this in one afternoon.'

'I'm adapting an old program. It'll work. You'll see.'

Sarah leaned close to his ear. 'I *will* see. Don't think I'm not onto you, Jacobs. You're a skiving little punk, and you're not focusing on the problem. But if you don't have something concrete to report soon, then you're going to regret it.'

Ryan swallowed. 'That's fair.'

As soon as she'd walked away, he closed down the code and pulled up some other software. He guessed he'd better have something to show the rest of the group.

Twenty minutes later, the cadets were called back to the centre of the room.

'It's time to report our findings,' said Mrs Tracey, glancing around. 'Marquez, Young, Zivai, talk to me about patterns.'

Jael looked tired. He pushed his glasses up his nose. 'There aren't any, ma'am. No statistically significant repeating ones, anyway. Only what you'd expect in this many numbers.'

Mrs Tracey frowned. 'How sure are you?'

'Ninety-nine percent. Lee, er, Cadet Young memorised the pages and he couldn't see any repeats. Zivai focused on one sheet and tried out nine different data transformations. I took several pages and looked for global patterns. The only weird thing was that some of the accounts seem to be missing.'

'Really?' Mrs Tracey looked uncomfortable.

'I'm not sure we've been given all the data. It's as though some of the rich people that lost money in the first place have been missed off the list.'

'Well, I can see you've been thorough. You're correct that we didn't give you all the data. There is a reason we are holding something back, but I can't disclose that to you now. How did the computer team get on? Do you agree with their conclusion?'

'Absolutely,' said Yu. 'There are no correlations or patterns between the accounts at all. The account numbers are as close to random as you can get.'

'The same is true for the IP addresses and devices,' added Sarah. 'There doesn't seem to be any connection between them. Anything to add, Jacobs?'

She looked pointedly at Ryan. Her eyes said it all: *You're a total waste of space.*

'No, I couldn't find any patterns either.'

She snorted. 'Well, there's a surprise.'

'So, the numbers aren't the answer,' concluded Mrs Tracey. 'How about the other groups? Any ideas why these individuals were chosen as targets or accomplices?'

'Just one,' offered Ranjit. 'There's an obvious disparity between the people who lost the money in the first place, and the people whose accounts they used at a later stage.'

'What do you mean?'

'Whoever the perpetrator is, they stole from very rich people. Those people seem to move in very similar circles. But the hacker used the accounts of, well, poor people, to move the money around.'

'I see.'

Ranjit felt brave enough to challenge the teacher. 'But, if you're holding some of the data back from us, then that may reveal other important connections.'

Some other cadets nodded, and Mrs Tracey hesitated as if she didn't know how to respond.

At that moment, Ryan saw something out of the corner of his eye that distracted him. Sarah was sitting just in front of him, on his left. On her back danced a red dot.

'Sarah, get down!' Ryan threw himself forward, knocking her off the stool and landing on top of her.

'What the hell do you think you're doing!' Sarah was livid. 'You're filthy! Get off me!'

'What's the meaning of this, Jacobs!' Mrs Tracey did not sound happy.

As Ryan looked up to answer her, he saw that with Sarah now out of the way, the dot rested on the teacher's breast.

'Mrs Tracey! Watch out!' Ryan pointed at the dot.

The teacher glanced down, bewildered. But even in her confusion, she registered the danger, and stepped aside at the crucial moment. There was the sound of shattering glass as one of the windows gave out, and a red beam of light shot through the room, narrowly missing her.

'Everyone out!' shouted Mrs Tracey, dashing for the door. She pressed a button on the intercom system. 'We have a Code Zero. Repeat: Code Zero. Initiate complete lockdown. Authorisation code nine alpha six two three.'

The cadets raced for the exit as several more windows shattered. Bright red laser-beams shot from one side of the room to the other.

Ryan and Sarah scrambled across the floor, staying as low as they could. Darting through a door, they hurtled down the staircase with the other terrified cadets. They finally came to a halt at the bottom of the stairwell, their backs to a wall.

Sarah glanced at Ryan, an unreadable expression on her face. Ryan wondered if she was about to thank him for saving her life.

'Jacobs,' she said, her voice cold. 'Don't EVER touch me again.'

12. DANGER

A siren blared through the academy.

Ryan followed the other cadets as they shuffled along the corridor to the sports hall. He looked nervously at the windows, feeling vulnerable. But he needn't have worried. Large metal shutters descended, shutting out the daylight as well as the danger.

An icy shiver ran down Ryan's spine. The school felt gloomy with the windows blocked off; it was even more like a prison than usual. He felt trapped, but at least they were safe.

As he shuffled into the drill hall, he felt stupid. All the other cadets wore their grey trousers and jackets, looking smart. He slid into place wearing his mud-spattered yellow and blue sports kit, looking like he'd been dragged through a hedge.

He tried to put it out of his mind. It was all part of the punishment. The colonel wanted to humiliate him, to make him stand out. And it was working. But he had bigger things to worry about right now.

The students stood to attention. Lady Devonmoor arrived and walked to the front. 'Good afternoon, everyone. I have some sad news. The academy is officially locked down. This is not a drill. For everyone's safety we will keep you all indoors.'

In a normal school, this kind of announcement would have caused a murmur of conversation, but the cadets at Devonmoor were too afraid to move or speak. Somehow, Ryan could still feel the tension in the room, as if everyone was holding their breath.

'I want to assure you that with the school in lockdown, you are safe. Isn't that right, Colonel?'

'It is.' The colonel stepped forward. 'It seems the intruder is equipped with a high-tech laser weapon, which was fired at cadets and teachers. However, this should not be a cause for alarm. Be assured that our soldiers will find and apprehend them. But at present, all outdoor activities are cancelled and the grounds are off limits. Is that understood?'

'YES, SIR.' The cadets spoke as one.

'You do not need to return to your last lesson of the day. You may instead begin your homework or evening activities. Dismissed.'

The cadets filed out in an orderly fashion, one line falling in behind another.

As soon as he reached the corridor, Ryan felt a hand on his shoulder and Sparks pulled him aside. They slipped into the empty changing rooms. The dim emergency lights barely gave off enough light to see.

'We have to tell them.' Sparks' voice quavered. 'We need to confess. Before anyone dies.'

'Are you crazy?' Ryan ran his hand through his messed-up hair. 'It's too late for that! It doesn't make a difference now. That thing shot at a teacher. It smashed up the academy. If they find out that we're involved, they'll give us a one-way ticket to Blackfell!'

'Maybe we deserve it,' said Sparks, miserably. He slumped onto a bench, his head in his hands.

'Don't say that! They don't have computers there. Do you think they'll have an engineering block? It'll just be cold showers and brutal exercise. And can you imagine who else is there? I'm a skinny runt and you're a fat kid. How long do you reckon we'll last?'

Sparks let out a moan.

'Look,' said Ryan, his voice softer. 'What difference does it make whether we tell them, anyway? They already know something dangerous is in the grounds and it has serious weapons. They locked the school down. Everyone is safe. They don't need to know we have anything to do with it. It doesn't change anything.'

'But if they knew what it was,' Sparks muttered, 'maybe they'd be better equipped to deal with it?'

'Maybe,' admitted Ryan. 'But we know it better than anyone and we can still get this under control. If we can work out why it's gone haywire, we could sort it. I just need some time in the computer lab. We will get through this, ok?'

Sparks nodded.

'Do you have another EMP blaster?' asked Ryan.

'No, that was the only one.'

'We'll need a way to disable the StealthBot long enough for me to access its programming once I've fixed the code. Can you find one?'

'I'll try to come up with something,' Sparks sniffed.

'That's more like it.' Ryan tried to sound cheerful, to jolly him along. 'Come on, we have some free time. Let's not waste it sitting here. I have to get to a computer.'

***

It didn't take long for Ryan to get in the zone.

Sitting at his favourite terminal in the ICT lab in the basement, he scrolled through the code looking for errors. Even with the school locked down, this room didn't feel any different; there was never any daylight in here.

With sports and some of the other extra-curricular activities off limits, several other cadets had settled in front of machines, killing time on the net. Their constant babble irritated Ryan, but they had as much right to be there as he did. If he was honest, he was jealous of them. They all looked so happy and relaxed in their clean uniforms. The biggest thing they had to worry about was homework.

Meanwhile, however many times he scanned the code, he couldn't see where he'd gone wrong. Maybe the issue was with Sparks' hardware after all. There was only one thing he could do. It was a risk, but one worth taking. He got up from his seat and sidled up to the door that led into Mr Davids' office. He knocked softly.

'Come in.'

Ryan pushed open the door, to discover Mr Davids immersed in a project of his own.

'Hi, sir.'

Mr Davids glanced over. 'Ah, Ryan, have you been playing football? Shouldn't you have changed?'

'No, sir. The colonel told me not to.'

'I see,' said Mr Davids, clearly not seeing at all. 'Well, I'm busy at the moment.'

That wasn't what Ryan wanted to hear, but he didn't give up. 'What are you working on?'

Most teachers would resent a student asking, but Mr Davids loved to talk about his work. 'Some final subroutines for the Chaos Flower. Your code works beautifully, by the way. I still don't know how you did it.'

Ryan smiled. 'Just a flash of inspiration I guess.'

The truth was he'd been injected with a brain-enhancing drug at the time, but the teacher didn't need to know that.

'Anyway,' said the teacher, peering at Ryan through his small round glasses, 'how can I help you?'

'I just wanted your advice. I'm working on something interesting. You'll like it. Maybe a bit later, if you're busy right now?'

'Give me ten minutes,' said the teacher.

'Thanks, sir.'

13. FREE

It wasn't ten minutes. It was over half an hour before Mr Davids emerged from his office and walked over to where Ryan was sitting. There was no point being annoyed: that was par for the course when you wanted help from a genius.

'So, what's this new project of yours?'

'Do you know much about Artificial Intelligence?' asked Ryan. Then he realised how patronising he sounded. 'Sorry, of course you do. I just meant, have you ever tried to design one before? For real?'

The teacher gave Ryan a strange look. 'Oh yes, many times. Complex field, my boy. Why do you ask? Is that what you have here?'

'Yeah, want to take a look?'

Mr Davids scrolled through the code, his eyes flicking between the commands with lightning speed. 'You have a lot of sensory inputs here. Where's that data coming from?'

'Oh, it's designed to function in a robot.'

'I see. This is an excellent program, Ryan. Very efficient.' He continued to familiarise himself with the code. 'So, what's the problem?'

'I wanted to check something with you, sir. The Asimov protocol. I'm not sure if it works correctly. Here, let me show you.' Ryan scrolled down to the right section.

'The Asimov protocol. Very good, very good.' Mr Davids looked amused. 'Based on the three laws of robotics I'm guessing?'

'Well, the first and third of them, anyway.'

'It can't harm humans. And it can defend itself, insofar as that doesn't lead it to harm any humans.'

'Yes, sir. They're the ones.'

'But you missed out the second law. The one that says the robot has to obey any commands it's given.'

'Yes, sir. I wanted the robot to make its own choices.'

'I see.' Mr Davids frowned a little as he read through the code. 'What effect did that have?'

'In the simulation I ran, the robot sometimes chose to, er, consider courses of action that might have led to a person being harmed.'

He didn't want the teacher to get suspicious or make any connection between his program and what had led to the school being locked down. But he needn't have worried. Mr Davids lived in his own digital world. He probably didn't even know about the attack.

'That's troubling. I wonder if it's related to you missing the second law.'

'How do you mean, sir?'

'You chose not to make the robot obey its commands because you wanted it to have personality. But how did you implement that in other parts of the program?'

'I gave it the opportunity to choose between options.'

'But machines don't have free-will, Ryan.'

'They could,' said Ryan, stubbornly. 'Why should they have to do everything we tell them? Why should they be our slaves?'

'It's not about that.' Mr Davids cocked his head to one side. 'It's simply about their nature. They follow their programming. That's what a robot does. So, how did you try to give it free-will? What kind of algorithm does that?'

'Look, I'll show you.' Ryan scrolled down again. It took a while to locate it, but then he stood back, crossing his arms. 'See?'

Mr Davids studied the code, his forehead creasing in concentration. 'A quantum possibility matrix. Clever. That would certainly simulate some high-level volition.'

'Simulate? I reckon it's the real thing, sir.'

'Hmm. I'd argue that it just inserts an element of random chance into the robot's decision-making procedures.'

'Well, maybe that's what happens in our brains.'

'Fair point,' allowed Mr Davids. Any other teacher would hate being contradicted; he seemed in his element. 'I can see you've thought hard about this, but either way, I think we've located your problem.'

'How so?'

'Well, whether it's random chance or free-will, by allowing the program to consider all possibilities and make its own choices, you've messed up the Asimov protocol. In effect, the robot can decide not to follow its instructions. Even the instruction about not harming people.'

Ryan stared at the teacher. 'You mean...'

'If you actually used this code, Ryan, you'd have a very dangerous robot on your hands.'

***

He'd been so stupid.

Why hadn't he just settled for a normal robot, one which did as it was told?

Way to go, Ryan.

It had felt so important to him that the robot could make its own choices, he'd let it ruin the entire project. He'd got so sick of following rules himself that he couldn't bear to make the robot do the same thing.

It's a robot, Ryan. Get a grip.

Devonmoor Academy was messing with his head.

He went through the code, line by line, ruthlessly erasing the quantum possibility matrix and any reference to it. By the time he was finished, this thing would be so obedient even the colonel wouldn't be able to find fault.

He took a break for dinner, but other than that he sat transfixed by the screen, tapping away at the keyboard.

Hours later, he finished.

He leaned back and tugged at his muddy socks. It was pointless, an act of habit; the sock ties already kept them up by his knees.

Which reminded him: he still had two hundred lines to do before morning. And it was nearly time for lights out.

Saving the revised code, and logging off, Ryan dashed back to his dormitory. Jael, Kev and Lee were getting ready for bed.

'Alright?' asked Kev. 'Where have you been all evening?'

'Computer lab.' Ryan shrugged. 'Just working on some code.'

'I don't know how you had the headspace to do that after the Forum,' said Lee. 'We analysed those numbers for hours. I'll be seeing them in my sleep.'

Jael shuddered. 'Don't, Lee. My head still hurts.'

The door to the room slammed open and Sarrell walked in. The boys all stood to attention, even though three of them were half-naked.

'Still in your kit, Jacobs?' Sarrell sneered, getting right up to Ryan's face.

'Of course.' Ryan glared back at Sarrell. One day he would get payback on the bully. But for now, he had to play along.

'Well, I'm just here to give you and your mates fair warning. I *will* come to check on you in the night. And if I find you've taken it off, then your whole dorm is going to be sharing your punishment. So, it's in all of your best interest to make sure Jacobs follows the rules. Do I make myself clear?'

The boys answered together. 'Yes, sir.'

'Good.' Sarrell turned to leave the room. 'It already smells bad in here. Imagine how bad it'll be by the end of the week.'

Ryan didn't want to think about it. The boys were going to hate him. But what could he do?

'Have a good night, boys.' Sarrell slammed the door as he went. Almost instantly the light went out, and they heard the lock click.

'I don't think that's an empty threat, Ryan,' said Kev, an edge to his voice. 'You're not gonna screw this up, are you?'

'Yeah,' added Jael. 'I don't want to be stuck in sports kit for a week.'

'Don't worry. I'll handle it.' Ryan reassured them. 'I'll sleep in it, just like the colonel wants.'

'Good.' Jael settled down, as Ryan grabbed a paper and pen from the drawer.

'What are you doing now?' asked Kev, confused.

'Two hundred lines,' admitted Ryan. 'I need them for tomorrow morning. I'll do them in the bathroom.'

'Couldn't you have done them earlier?' groaned Jael.

'He's right, Ryan. Why did you leave them until now?' asked Kev. 'Sometimes I don't know what's worse: what the colonel does to you or what you do to yourself.'

'It's alright,' said Ryan. 'It won't make a difference to you guys.'

He headed into the tiny bathroom and closed the door. Then he slumped to the floor, his leg pressed against the side of the toilet. It would be hard to imagine a more uncomfortable position to write in. But he didn't have much choice. The light in the main bedroom would turn off any minute now.

I am lazy, cheating scum and I deserve to be punished.

I am lazy, cheating scum and I deserve to be punished.

I am lazy, cheating scum and I deserve to be punished.

By the time he'd written two sides, he realised just how long it was going to take. He stifled a yawn and carried on. He had to get it done.

I am lazy, cheating scum and I deserve to be punished.

I am lazy, cheating scum...

14. NIGHT

He awoke to the sound of the toilet being flushed. He was lying on the bathroom floor, dribble running down his chin. Halfway through the lines, he must have fallen asleep.

He looked up, expecting to see one of his roommates. Instead, Sarrell stood there, smirking.

'Shh,' said the prefect. 'Don't wake the others. Shouldn't you be standing to attention?'

Ryan clambered to his feet. 'I'm still in the kit.'

'I can see that. How are the lines going?'

'I've nearly finished.'

'Have you?' Sarrell cocked his head on one side, inches from Ryan's face. There was barely room for both of them in the tiny bathroom. 'Remind me what it was you had to write.'

'I am lazy, cheating scum and I deserve to be punished.'

'How many times do you have to write it?'

'Two hundred.'

'Well, hadn't you better make a start?'

'But I have, it's...' Ryan glanced down. The lines had gone.

'I don't see them, Jacobs.' Sarrell looked around, dramatically. 'Any idea where they could be?'

Ryan could hear the toilet cistern refilling.

Surely, he couldn't have...

Seeing the look on Sarrell's face, he knew it was true. The older boy had flushed them.

And the worst part was: he'd never be able to prove it. He clenched his jaw and stared at the bathroom wall.

'Nothing to say, Jacobs?'

'No.'

'No, *sir.*'

Ryan sighed. 'No, sir.'

'Well, it's only four in the morning, so you still have time to get the lines done. I wouldn't want to be in your shoes if you haven't completed them by the time you report to Sergeant Wright. If you were allowed any shoes, that is.'

Sarrell put his heavy boot on Ryan's socked foot and pressed down hard. Ryan pulled a face, but didn't make any sound.

'Carry on, Jacobs.'

As soon as Sarrell had left the bathroom, Ryan slumped back down. That boy was going to destroy him.

Picking up his pen, he started afresh.

I am lazy, cheating scum and I deserve to be punished.

His stomach felt tense, but he was too tired to hold on to the anger. After a while, he grew numb to the pain inside.

I am lazy, cheating scum and I deserve to be punished.

Every line hurt. Every line was an accusation. A confession. A revelation.

I am lazy, cheating scum and I deserve to be punished.

As he wrote it, tears formed in his eyes and he brushed them away with his dirty sleeve.

I am lazy, cheating scum and I deserve to be punished.

He began to wonder if it was true.

***

Ryan made his way to the gym in the darkness, his muddy trainers in his hands. He almost hadn't bothered to bring them, but didn't want to give Sergeant Wright any reason to increase his punishment. Not after he'd spent the rest of the night writing lines.

Despite the early hour, he felt strangely upbeat. With the academy in lockdown, at least he wouldn't have to do the run. He may have to do laps of the sports hall, or possibly spend time on a running machine, but either of those was better than having to run through the cold, dark woods with a killer robot on the loose.

He yawned as he pushed through the double doors that led to the sports department. He knocked on the door to Sergeant Wright's office.

It flung open; the sergeant seemed annoyed at being disturbed.

'I brought the lines, sir.' Ryan held them out. Behind the sergeant, he could see a soldier. He'd interrupted an important meeting.

'Wait for me in the sports hall, cadet. Stand to attention.'

'Yes, sir.'

The sergeant screwed up the lines without even looking at them and threw them in the bin as he closed the door.

What a complete waste of time.

It was deliberate. All part of the torture.

He yawned as he waited. He'd only got a few hours sleep, dozing on the bathroom floor. It was going to be hard to stay awake all day. The rest of the cadets weren't even up yet.

The large clock on the wall seemed to move in slow motion. As he couldn't do the run, he wondered if the sergeant would make him stand here for the entire hour, or even longer. It was tempting to lean against the wall, or to sit down, but there were cameras and the sergeant might be watching.

After half an hour had passed, the door banged open and Sergeant Wright strode in.

Ryan tensed, waiting for abuse.

'I bet you're feeling pretty pleased with yourself?'

'Sir?'

'I know what you're thinking. You must be ecstatic the academy is in lockdown. That way you get to skive cross-country yet again. Well, we can't have that, Jacobs, can we?'

'No, sir.'

'I just had news from the guards that they have completed a thorough search of the grounds. Whoever was in there has vanished. They left behind some old melted gun. It looked like it had exploded or something. Must have overheated.'

The EMP blaster. They thought that was the laser that had been used to fire at the school!

'So, they have given us the all-clear. We're no longer in lockdown. Which means, Jacobs, you get to do your run. Six miles, wasn't it?'

'Yes, sir.' His mouth felt dry. 'Are you sure it's safe?'

'Completely. The soldiers carried out a full scan using top-end equipment. If anyone or anything was out there, it would have shown up. You're not getting out of this.'

As the sergeant spoke, there was a whirring, clanking noise as the shutters over all the windows started to rise. It was still dark outside, so made little difference to the light in the gym.

'There, you see? Nothing to worry about, cadet. Apart from what will happen to you if you're not back here in fifty minutes. You've gone pale, Jacobs. Not feeling so cocky today? You've got another six days of this.' He sniffed the air near Ryan's shoulder. 'I sure feel sorry for your roommates.'

It wasn't the time limit that bothered him. Or the stinking kit. What Sergeant Wright didn't know was that the robot had been designed to evade detection using heat-mapping, radar and other technologies. That was why it was called the StealthBot. The soldiers might be sure that the grounds were safe, but they were wrong.

The robot was still out there.

And they were sending him into the woods.

Unarmed and alone.

15. WOODS

He pulled on his trainers, his legs shaking.

Sparks had been right. They should have owned up. Because they'd stayed quiet, no-one knew they were in danger. At any point, the StealthBot could open fire on the school. And this time, it might kill a student. Or a teacher. And it would all be Ryan's fault.

He felt sick as he set off, the flashlight on his headband illuminating the football pitch ahead. The freezing air shocked him awake, helping him think more clearly.

It would be madness to run through the woods. The cross-country route took him around the lake, right past the place where they'd last seen the StealthBot. But what other option did he have? If he tried to cheat, Sarrell would be waiting.

Any punishment is better than death.

So, why was he still running? And how long could they hold out? At some point they'd have to come clean.

But now he knew why the robot had malfunctioned, Ryan knew he could fix it. As long as

Sparks had found another way to disable it, he could reprogram it. Then everything would be ok.

He just had to hope the robot didn't kill anyone before that.

Especially him.

It had rained overnight, and the path was treacherous. He grimaced as his trainers splashed through the mud. Six miles of this. Every day. And why?

I am lazy, cheating scum and I deserve to be punished.

Was he ever going to get those words out of his head?

He could taste metal in his throat. Drips of water fell from the trees above as the wind blew through the branches. He leapt over a ditch.

And then he stopped.

He looked at the dark path ahead.

Come on, Ryan.

The odds of him encountering the StealthBot were practically zero. Last time, he and Sparks had been hunting it. Today, he would try to avoid it. Besides, the soldiers had been patrolling the grounds all night, and they hadn't seen it.

That's what his head said, but his feet wouldn't budge. He couldn't go any further. He had to stay this side of the lake, where it felt safe.

It was stupid. The StealthBot could have moved by now. It probably had. There was no reason to believe that one part of the woods was more dangerous than another. But every time Ryan had seen the red flashing light it had been in the same place, and there was no way he was going anywhere near there.

That meant he had to cheat.

Again.

If they caught him, he'd be for it, but at least he'd be alive.

He wouldn't cut through the school. Sarrell might be waiting. But if he stuck to the woods this side of the lake, no-one would ever suspect. Normally, prefects monitored the cadets when they did a run, but today he was alone. Surrounded by trees, there was no way anyone could see him.

He could do this.

He left the muddy path and forced a way through the undergrowth. Thick brambles dragged at his rugby shirt and scratched his legs, but he pushed on, ignoring the pain. He guessed this was why no-one came this way. You had to risk too many thorns and stinging nettles. But it was still better to get scratched than cut in half with a laser.

He emerged from the brambles into a small clearing. As he stepped forwards, the ground sucked at his feet, stagnant mud spilling over the sides of his trainers.

Ryan cursed, taking it one step at a time. If he got stuck in this marshland, then it was over. He could drown in this muck and no-one would ever know. In a hundred years time some archaeologist would dig up the body of a thirteen-year-old boy who was stupid enough to take a shortcut.

But the mud didn't get much deeper. It just smelt revolting, like rotten cabbage.

He groaned as he remembered he wasn't allowed to change. He had to wear these socks for the rest of the week. No-one would want to go near him.

One problem at a time, Ryan.

He pulled himself up onto firmer ground, skirting around the last of the bog. It couldn't be much further.

His trainers squelched as he walked, brown liquid oozing out of the sides.

He paused as he saw something up ahead in the flashlight beam. It didn't look like a tree, but it wasn't a robot either. He moved towards it, holding his breath.

A chain-link fence. Two metres high, topped with barbed wire.

This was why Sergeant Wright knew he wouldn't cheat by taking a shortcut through the woods. There was no way through.

And now, even if he risked running around the lake, he didn't stand a chance of making it back in time. He'd wasted too much time walking in the wrong direction through brambles and bog.

His pain and effort had all been for nothing.

He was totally screwed.

Ryan had no desire to trudge back the way he had come. He figured he might as well head along the fence, back towards the school, and take whatever punishment Sergeant Wright dished out. How much worse could it get?

As he contemplated that, there was a noise up ahead.

Ryan froze.

There it was again. Something was rustling through the bushes, heading in his direction. He switched off the light and dived into the weeds, lying on his belly on the damp ground. He cursed as stinging nettles brushed against the top of his legs, and they began to smart.

Was it a soldier? Or was it...

The StealthBot.

The eye looked brighter than before in the darkness, casting an eerie red glow on Ryan's surroundings.

Thankfully, it was on the other side of the fence, so Ryan was safe. At least, that's what he thought at first.

The black plate on the robot's chest slid open to reveal a circular saw which extended out and started cutting the wire mesh, sparks flying in every direction. Any moment now the robot would be through, only metres from where Ryan was lying in the dirt.

Ryan looked behind him. There was nowhere to go. His best hope was to wait it out. He didn't think he could move anyway; he was too afraid.

The robot had finished cutting; its massive arms pulled the wire mesh apart. It stepped through and stood for a moment, swivelling from side to side, scanning the area. Ryan lay still.

Would it know he was here?

As if answering the question, the robot spoke.

'THREAT DETECTED.'

Perhaps he should say something. Maybe he could reason with it, try to persuade it not to kill him. He opened his mouth, but no sound came out.

He wondered if anyone would miss him when he'd gone, or whether they'd just be glad to rid of a troublemaker.

His parents would be sorry. They'd regret leaving him here at the academy. It served them right.

But really, it was all his own fault. If he hadn't made the mistake with the program, none of this would be happening.

It was because he'd messed up that he was about to die.

The robot lifted its heavy arm and pointed its laser in his direction.

Ryan's heart was in his throat.

This was it.

He tried to think up a plan, any plan to escape.

But there was no time.

The robot fired.

16. ALIVE

He glanced up.

Somehow, he was alive.

For a moment, he wondered if the laser had sliced through his body and his brain still hadn't registered the pain. It would come, any moment now.

'THREAT NEUTRALISED.'

The robot turned away and stomped off into the woods. Ryan waited for what felt like an age, lying in the nettles, wondering what had happened.

Eventually, he hauled himself to his feet. His legs shook violently, and he grabbed one of the tree trunks for support. He threw up, emptying his stomach on the muddy ground.

Had the robot missed? It didn't seem likely. This was a high-tech military-grade piece of hardware and it was shooting from point-blank range.

What, then?

As he looked around, he found the answer.

Lying on the ground behind him was a smoking pile of fur. It looked like it had once been a rabbit.

'Sorry, little fella,' muttered Ryan, 'but I'm sure glad it was you, and not me.'

He was grateful for one other thing: there was now a hole in the fence. He stepped through, taking care not to touch it in case it was still hot.

He sprinted off, keen to get as far away from the robot as possible.

Heading around this side of the lake cut miles off his route. If he kept moving, he could make it back in time.

His legs itched where the nettles had stung them, but he smiled as he realised it would have been worse if his socks hadn't been pulled up. 'Maybe you're right, Sergeant Wright,' he muttered to himself, 'maybe it does matter.'

Now he just had to get back to the school.

This wasn't over.

The StealthBot was still in the grounds and could fire on the school at any moment.

He had to hope that Sparks had come up with some way to catch it.

***

'Morning, Sparks.' Ryan placed his tray on the table next to the overweight cadet and sat down, his two slices of toast looking pathetic next to Sparks' cooked breakfast.

Unfortunately, the boys weren't able to chat freely as Lee, Jael and Ayana sat nearby.

'Do you have to sit with us, Ryan?' Jael held his nose as he caught a whiff of the stagnant ditch water.

'Leave him alone,' cut in Lee. 'It's not his fault. We stick with each other. Don't let the colonel break us up.'

'I was only joking,' said Jael defensively. Ryan wasn't sure that was true.

'How long have you been wearing that now?' asked Ayana.

'Just over a day. I have another six to go.'

'That is so harsh.' She shook her head.

'It's also pretty clever,' added Jael. 'After this, even Ryan will make sure he wears the right stuff.'

It was true. They were wearing him down, forcing him to follow the rules.

'And Lee said you have to do a run every day as well?'

'Yep, the full six miles.' Ryan took another bite of his toast. 'But you know me, I like a challenge.'

Lee laughed, milk spurting out his nose. 'You're a legend.'

'Maybe. But I'm also shattered. I was up all night writing lines. Being a rebel isn't as much fun as it looks.'

Jael had little sympathy. 'That was your own fault. You didn't need to leave them that late.' He had no idea that Ryan had spent most of the previous evening trying to fix the robot's code. He also didn't know that Sarrell had made Ryan do them all again in the middle of the night.

'I just forgot,' lied Ryan. 'Anyway, Sparks, did you have any luck with that problem you were working on?' He couldn't wait any longer for an answer, and knew the others wouldn't have any clue what he was talking about.

'Yes,' said Sparks, giving Ryan a meaningful look. 'I had a breakthrough. I'll tell you about it later.'

That was exactly what Ryan wanted to hear.

***

After breakfast, Ryan pulled Sparks aside and told him of his encounter in the woods.

'You did the right thing, staying still. The robot focuses on movement more than anything else. If you ever face it again, don't move.'

'Trust me, I won't. So, what's the plan?'

'Well, I figure no weapon is going to work, however high-tech,' said Sparks. 'Now we know it shoots at people, if we wander through the woods with a gun, the chances are we're gonna get fried.'

'True,' allowed Ryan. 'But how do we stop it?'

'By my calculations, it's battery will be low. Around five o'clock today, finding power will be a priority. And it's not going to find any out there in the woods.'

Ryan looked up in horror. 'Do you think it will break into the school?'

'No,' said Sparks. 'Not the main school building, anyway. The most likely scenario is that it will return to the one place it knows it can get charged. The place where it was created.'

'The engineering block?'

'Exactly. And once it's plugged in, I plan to overload the circuit. That should shut it down.'

'That is genius,' admitted Ryan, 'and it doesn't sound too risky.'

'We just have to hope there's no more trouble between now and then,' said Sparks. 'If the school gets locked down, we won't be able to make it to the warehouse to mess with the power.'

'True.' Ryan hadn't thought of that.

'Do we know what went wrong yet?' added Sparks. 'Have you checked the program?'

Ryan looked away, embarrassed. 'Yeah, my bad. I gave it a little too much personality I'm afraid. That allowed it to break its programming, and choose not to obey the Asimov protocol.'

Sparks had been right, but he wasn't going to rub it in. 'Have you sorted it?'

'Sure. I've been through that code line by line. By the time I upload the new program, it's going to be more obedient than Sarah Devonmoor.'

Sparks chuckled. 'That would be quite an achievement.'

'Anyway, we need to get to the Forum. We don't want to keep Mrs Tracey waiting.'

'Oh, you haven't heard?'

'Heard what?'

'Mrs Tracey isn't leading it today. Colonel Keller is taking over.'

'You're not serious?' Ryan couldn't bear the thought of an entire day with the colonel.

'Yeah, and while they fix the room upstairs, we have to meet in his classroom.'

'Well, that's sure gonna be fun.'

17. RESULTS

Colonel Keller's classroom was one of the most depressing places in the academy. There were no chairs or tables. Neither were there any signs or noticeboards. The only relief from the plain khaki-green walls was a line of windows overlooking the school playing fields. Ryan glanced outside, wondering if the StealthBot was out there, somewhere in the trees beyond.

There were some markings on the floor, showing cadets where they should stand. Ryan walked to one of them and stood to attention, in line with the other students. The colonel stood on the stage, looming over them like a gorilla preparing to attack.

'At ease, cadets.' He looked around the room. 'Well, well, what a sorry bunch of cadets they've picked this time. When Mrs Tracey informed me you hadn't had any luck working on the problem, I wondered why. But now, I think I know. We decided that a different approach might yield better results.'

The cadets knew better than to say anything. The colonel was just warming up. He always liked to start with insults.

'What on earth is that smell? Oh wait, that must be you, Jacobs.'

Keep calm, Ryan. He's just trying to wind you up.

'Yes, sir.'

'Feeling privileged that you don't have to keep changing back into your uniform?'

'Yes, sir.' He hated it, but the colonel knew that.

'Well, for what it's worth, I'm glad to have you here.'

Ryan tensed. He wasn't used to receiving compliments from the colonel. He stayed silent.

'After all, this is right up your street isn't it? Hacking into people's accounts and stealing money? I mean, isn't that the sort of criminal activity you enjoy?'

'I guess so.'

'I think that makes you something of an expert in this, so I will expect great things from you this morning. Given your background, I'm surprised that you didn't come up with anything yesterday.'

Ryan couldn't hold back any longer. 'Well, it might help if I didn't have to get up at six to do a stupid run! I'm too tired to think!'

The colonel let out a snort of derision. 'That's right, Jacobs, blame everyone else as usual. I'm sure I don't need to remind you *why* you have to do a run every morning?'

Ryan glared back.

Sarah Devonmoor took a small step forward. 'Permission to speak, sir?'

'Permission granted.'

'Jacobs wasn't focused on the task yesterday. I think he couldn't be bothered.'

Thanks for ratting on me, Sarah.

'Is that so? Well, people like Jacobs don't do things because they are *supposed* to. They only do them if they're *made* to. But don't worry, I will find ways to motivate him, won't I, Jacobs?'

Ryan swallowed and looked away. He forced out the words the colonel wanted to hear. 'Yes, sir.'

'Good.' The colonel stepped back and his eyes swept across the room. 'Since your failure to make any progress yesterday, there has been a fresh development. The Outlier has sent a message, claiming responsibility for the thefts.'

There was a sharp intake of breath. Students knew of the Outlier, but all they'd heard was rumours. He'd been a student at Devonmoor, before he went rogue. The teachers rarely talked about him.

'The Outlier was one of the most intelligent students who ever attended this academy. He was also one of the most egotistical, rebellious and selfish students we ever had.' The colonel's lip curled. 'He was almost as bad as Jacobs.'

There were a few sniggers around the room. A couple of people glanced in Ryan's direction.

'Things did not go well for the Outlier at this school. He couldn't demonstrate the level of discipline needed. By the time he left, he felt bitter and angry. Now, he wants revenge.'

Ryan could understand that. After he'd spent a few years here, he'd probably feel the same way.

'In his message to Lady Devonmoor, he admitted that he stole millions from her investment accounts. He made certain demands, and unless we meet those demands, he said he would continue to strip her estate of funds, leaving her destitute.'

Ranjit braved a question. 'What were the demands, sir?'

'Those are confidential, cadet. There is a lot of history between the Outlier and this school, and I cannot share it with you today. But, needless to say, we will not be complying with them.'

Ranjit looked like he wanted to object. Without full knowledge of the Outlier's motivations, it was hard to predict his next movements. But he knew better than to contradict the colonel.

'But sir,' said Jael, 'we were given loads of data about the victims and Lady Devonmoor wasn't on the list.'

'We didn't equip you with all the data when you began your investigation,' admitted the colonel. 'As you will imagine, losing that amount of money was an embarrassment to Lady Devonmoor. There was no need to advertise it to the cadets at this academy. However, since then, the situation has changed. Things have got personal.'

'How?' That was the younger cadet, the outspoken kid.

'This may be an unusual lesson, cadet, but you will still address me as "sir" or you will be doing push ups until you puke.'

The cadet turned white. He didn't repeat the question. He didn't need to: Jael had worked out the answer.

'Was it because of the attack on the school, sir?'

'Yes, Marquez. The Outlier knows all about the Forum. He will be fully aware that students from this academy will try to stop him. We think that he or one of his henchmen snuck into the grounds and opened fire on you all to distract you, or...' The colonel hesitated, looking as if he was about to say something else. He glanced over at Sarah.

Ryan couldn't help thinking they weren't being given all the facts. Regardless, the teachers were wrong. The attack on the school had nothing to do with the Outlier. They were blaming the former cadet for something he hadn't done.

'But, sir, that still doesn't explain why other accounts had money stolen from them,' said Yu, looking confused. 'If he's just out to get Lady Devonmoor, why target so many other people as well?'

'We're not sure,' admitted the colonel. 'But it seems likely it's to add to the pressure. Most of the accounts are of people linked to the family or the school. If we don't give in to his demands, it's not just Lady Devonmoor that will suffer, anyone connected to her will go down as well.'

'So, what do we do, sir?'

'This morning, I will split you into two groups. One group will report to Dr Torren's classroom. A great deal of material has been amassed there on the

Outlier, from old school reports to psychological assessments. Some of it has been withheld or redacted for reasons of confidentiality, but there is plenty that should give you an insight into his personality, and how he likes to work. Perhaps we can use that information to manipulate him, or locate him. The other group will comprise the more technically skilled cadets: Devonmoor, Yu, Sparks. You are going to spend the morning in the computer lab, trying to create a program which simulates what the Outlier is doing.'

'Sir, you forgot Jacobs,' pointed out Sarah.

'Ah no, Jacobs is going to be staying here with me. I have a special job for him. And Cadet Young, you can stay behind as well.'

Lee looked bewildered, but hung back as the cadets filtered out. Ryan caught his eye.

Why did the colonel want them to stay behind?

Whatever the reason, it wouldn't be good.

18. HACK

Colonel Keller waited until all the other students had left, then stood in front of Ryan.

'Your days of slacking are over, Jacobs. Fetch a laptop from the computer labs. You have two minutes. MOVE!'

Ryan dashed off, his socked feet sliding on the polished floor as he skidded out of the classroom. When he arrived at the computer room, there was no sign of Mr Davids, so he grabbed one of the laptop bags from the corner.

He ran back, wondering what the colonel was going to make him do. At least a computer was involved. He'd be on his territory. How bad could it be?

When he returned, Lee was standing to attention. Colonel Keller had set up a folding table by the windows. 'Put it here and plug it in.'

Ryan did as he was told, his hands fumbling with the power cable.

'Get on with it, Jacobs. Stop stalling. I thought you liked computers.'

'I do, sir.' Ryan got it set up and switched it on. 'It'll take a minute or two to boot up.' Outside, the sky had turned dark. Ominous clouds gathered overhead. He could see the woods at the other end of the football pitch. He wondered if the StealthBot was there, watching.

'Get on the floor, cadet.'

'Sir?'

'The plank position. Now.'

Ryan dropped down as if he was going to do press-ups, but with his elbows on the ground. He held his torso in the air, his muscles tense. The colonel stood in front of him, so close that Ryan could see his reflection in the shiny black boots.

Don't break, Ryan.

'You will know computers are not exactly my area of expertise.' The colonel spoke slowly, enjoying Ryan's discomfort. 'However, you are one of the best hackers in the country, or so Mr Davids claims. Just like the Outlier.'

'Yes, sir.'

'And the Outlier has hacked into thousands of bank accounts over the last few weeks. So, I imagine you must be able to do the same, if you wanted to?'

Just how stupid was this man?

'No, sir,' Ryan gasped. 'It's not that easy.'

'I didn't ask if it was easy, Jacobs. I asked if it was possible. And as he can do it, it must be possible, mustn't it?'

'Yes, sir.' Ryan still couldn't see how it could be done, but he didn't feel it would be wise to contradict the colonel.

'You're going to show me just how hard it is this morning. And I may not know much about computers, but I know about dealing with lazy, skiving cadets like you. You are going to hack into a bank account. Just one. And the longer it takes, the worse things will get for you and your friend. Do you understand?'

'Y-Yes, sir.' Ryan couldn't hold the plank position for much longer. Any moment now he was going to collapse.

'Get up.'

Ryan clambered to his feet and glanced over at the computer. 'Shall I fetch a chair from next door, sir?'

'A chair?' The colonel smirked. 'No, Jacobs. Lazy cadets don't get chairs else they slack off. You can stay standing.'

For the whole morning?

Outside, the wind was picking up and rain started to fall in giant drops. Ryan hoped that somehow it might prevent the StealthBot from attacking the school, but it wasn't likely to make a difference. Sparks would hardly design a robot that couldn't function in the rain.

He walked over to the laptop and logged in. 'Before I get started, I just need to download some software. Whose account do you want me to hack?'

'That's easy,' said the colonel. 'Find one belonging to Matilda Jane Devonmoor.'

Ryan swivelled around in shock. 'Lady Devonmoor?'

'Yes, cadet. Is that a problem?'

'Won't I get into trouble?' Ryan had fallen foul of Colonel Keller's schemes before. He couldn't help wondering if this was just another attempt to get him expelled.

'As if you care.' The colonel looked amused. 'I thought you enjoyed being punished?'

Ryan turned back to the screen. What could he do? If it was a trap, he'd have to explain that he'd only hacked into the account under direct instructions from the colonel. Surely, even at Devonmoor, he shouldn't be punished for that?

'Do you have the account numbers?' asked Ryan.

'No. Do you?' The colonel raised his eyebrows. He wasn't going to make this any easier.

'I can find them, but it'll take longer.'

'That's not my problem.' The colonel stood at his shoulder. Ryan could smell his breath: a foul aroma of half-digested bacon and strong coffee. 'It is, however, a problem you will want to solve quickly. Cadet Young, take off your jacket.'

Lee looked nervous. He unzipped his top and removed it. The colonel took it from him and threw it aside. Lee looked a lot younger, standing there in his vest.

'What's wrong, cadet? Not in the mood to kick me today?'

'No, sir.' Lee looked scared. The colonel still hadn't forgiven him for trying to boot him in the privates when he was suffering from the Fury.

The colonel walked over to a door that led from the classroom out to the sports field. As he opened it, a freezing wind blew into the room. 'Your job is simple, cadet. You're going to do laps of the football pitch. Every time you get to the goal mouth at this end, do ten press-ups and ten sit-ups. You can go slow, but if you stop, you'll regret it.'

Lee trembled in the doorway. 'Yes, sir.'

'You'll no doubt be wondering how long you'll be out there. Well, you're not coming back in until Jacobs here has hacked into the account.'

'That's not fair!' shouted Ryan. 'It could take hours!'

'Well, Jacobs, if you care about your friend you'll want to do it a lot quicker than that.'

'But he'll get hypothermia!'

'Not if he keeps running.'

***

'He's not looking very happy,' mused the colonel.

Ryan glanced up. The rain was torrential now and Lee was jogging dejectedly across the pitch. He was holding his arms across his chest in a vain attempt to keep warm, the water hammering against his skinny body. He'd been out there for over an hour and didn't look like he could take much more.

Ryan wanted to swear at the colonel, but he knew that Lee would only suffer as a result. 'Please, sir. Let him in. I'm going as fast as I can.'

The colonel laughed. 'He's a big boy, Jacobs. He can handle it. Besides, it might toughen him up.'

You're just like Sarrell.

Ryan turned his attention to the hack. He'd located one of Lady Devonmoor's investment accounts, but getting access required cracking a password as well as a PIN. It was slow work. Ryan had a spreadsheet open and was comparing the results of the "DataDrill" application's efforts, trying to draw some conclusions.

'There's something I don't understand, sir,' admitted Ryan, running his hand through his hair. 'Why don't you just get Mr Davids and the other teachers on to this. Why bother with the Forum of students at all? I mean, however good we are, we're not as good as the teachers.'

'Typical. You expect the teachers to do all the work?'

'No, sir. I didn't mean that. But Mr Davids could do this even faster than me.'

'As it happens, Jacobs, some of the teachers do also work on the problems when a Forum is called. That way we have twice as much chance of solving it.'

So, Mr Davids was working on this problem as well. Maybe he would have more luck than Ryan.

Outside, Lee had dropped to the ground and was forcing his body up and down, his vest and trousers clinging to his body.

Ryan squinted at the screen. Even with this amount of data, he knew it would be hours before he had the password, let alone the PIN code.

'I can't do it.' He sighed and turned to the colonel. 'The password is double-encrypted. It doesn't matter what you do to Lee. Or what you threaten me with. It won't change the facts. Breaking into this account will take days.'

'Interesting.' The colonel looked out at Lee, then back at Ryan. 'Even though your friend is suffering, there's no way you can speed the process up?'

'No, sir. Bank accounts are super-secure. Especially with investments like these. It can't be done.'

Ryan wasn't expecting the colonel to listen, but to his surprise, the man walked over to the door.

'CADET YOUNG, GET BACK IN HERE!'

Lee didn't need telling twice. He dashed over, almost collapsing on the classroom floor, his teeth chattering.

'I'm so sorry, Lee,' said Ryan, feeling guilty.

'Head back to your dorm room, cadet,' said the colonel. 'Take a long, hot shower and get changed. Then report back here.'

Lee grabbed his jacket and ran off, looking relieved.

'So, what happens now?' asked Ryan.

'Fetch the others,' ordered the colonel. 'We have work to do.'

19. FAIL

'So, what did you achieve?'

For the first time, Sarah looked flustered. 'Well, sir, we tried to come up with an algorithm that would identify suitable accounts to be used for transfers, but even that was tricky. So, if I'm honest, not a lot.'

The colonel looked like he was about to explode. But even he didn't dare pick on Lady Devonmoor's granddaughter.

Must be nice to get special treatment, thought Ryan.

'Cadet Jeet, your group better have something for me? Or are the lot of you a useless waste of space?'

'No, sir. I mean, yes, sir.' Ranjit stepped forward. 'We drew several conclusions about the Outlier's methods. It might have been easier if so much of the information hadn't been withheld.'

The colonel glared at him. 'We decide what you need to know. Do you have a problem with that?'

'No, sir.' Ranjit looked away, not daring to object. 'It surprised us to discover the Outlier came from a rich family. His real name was Sam Novak, and he grew up wealthy and privileged. So, it seems strange that he's targeting people like that now. It's not like he's from the other side of the tracks; he was a spoilt rich kid himself.'

'He certainly was,' agreed the colonel. 'But he was also a traitor. He's doing this partly out of spite and partly so we submit to his demands.'

'That sounds likely. His psychological reports show he has Oppositional Defiant Disorder. He's hard-wired to break the rules and challenge authority. The more he was punished during his time here, the more he acted out. That's why he hates the school so much.'

'I told you that already.' The colonel was growing impatient.

'Yes, but one thing that was especially interesting was that he got into trouble a lot for his inability to work in a team. He always preferred working alone. He thought he was better than everyone else.' As Ranjit said this, Sarah looked over at Ryan and raised her eyebrows. He ignored her as Ranjit carried on. 'He had huge trust issues. So, it isn't likely he's working with anyone else right now. It's not a conspiracy, and he hasn't assembled a team of hackers. This is something he's doing alone.'

'An interesting point,' allowed the colonel. 'But Jacobs here has made it clear to me just how long it would take him to break into just one bank account, let alone thousands.'

'That's what doesn't make sense, sir. The Outlier didn't like to work hard. He was a genius with computers, but even with that he made sloppy errors in his attempt to cut corners.'

'I remember,' said the colonel. 'He was a lazy delinquent. Well, Jacobs, sound like anyone you know?'

Ryan felt his face burn. 'Sure, sir. It sounds like me. I get it. But I don't see how that helps. I'm not the Outlier.'

'But Ryan, don't you see?' Ranjit stared at him as if it were obvious. 'You're the key. If we want to know how the Outlier is doing this, all we need to do is ask ourselves how *you* would do it.'

Ryan didn't like where this was going. 'The colonel already tried that. It didn't go so well. I couldn't hack into one bank account in an hour, let alone thousands. Do you know how hard that is?'

'No,' said Ranjit. 'But you do. And someone as lazy as you wouldn't spend days doing it. So, there must be another way. There's something buried deep in your head that is the key to all this. You're like a carbon copy of the Outlier, just a bit younger. You can solve this if you put your mind to it.'

'An interesting point, Cadet Jeet,' agreed the colonel. 'Do the rest of you concur?'

The other cadets either shrugged or nodded.

'Well,' said the colonel, turning back to Ryan, 'that gives us another impossible challenge. We need to see if we can drag something out of that tiny little brain of yours.'

***

Ryan was alone with the colonel. The others had been sent for a break. He wasn't allowed one of those.

'So, Jacobs, we have a dilemma on our hands. All the other cadets believe you can solve the mystery of how the Outlier is gaining access to so many accounts. You, however, refuse to co-operate.'

'That's not fair. I'm trying.'

'How badly do you want to get to the answer, Jacobs? How desperate are you to work it out?'

Ryan shrugged. 'Pretty desperate, I guess.'

'*Pretty* desperate? Is that like *sort of* bothered? Are we perhaps taking up too much of your valuable time? Do you have other places you need to be?'

'No, sir.'

Just catching a killer robot.

'Well, I'm going to help you focus. Do you know what helps people focus more than anything else?'

Ryan couldn't stop himself. 'Chocolate ice cream?'

To his surprise, the colonel laughed. 'It's good that you've got a sense of humour, Jacobs. Let's see if you're still feeling as cocky in an hour's time. The thing that helps people focus is pain. Or the threat of it.'

It would be, wouldn't it?

'Fetch your trainers.'

Ryan groaned as he collected his muddy trainers from outside the classroom. There was only one reason he'd need these. He was going outside.

'You're going to pick up where Cadet Young left off. Keep running around the football field. Ten push ups and ten sit-ups every time you reach the far end.'

Ryan looked out at the torrential rain, hurling itself at the window and bouncing off the path.

'How many laps, sir?'

'As many as it takes to come up with answers. If you stop, your whole dorm will end up out there with you. Don't come back until you have some kind of breakthrough.' The colonel opened the door and Ryan felt the rain blow into his face. 'Want to make any more smart remarks?'

'No, sir.'

'I thought not.'

Taking a deep breath, Ryan ran out into the storm.

20. FIELD

His legs ached. His lungs screamed. The heavy rugby shirt clung to his body, cold and wet.

He glanced over at the school, desperate to be back inside. Up and down the pitch he ran, the rain cascading from his hair and streaming down his face.

He'd tucked his hands into his sleeves, but didn't dare to pull the socks up over his knees. That would get him in even worse trouble. That left his legs exposed to the icy wind.

He approached the far side of the pitch, glancing nervously into the trees. Running laps in this weather would be harsh enough without the threat of being zapped by a killer robot. The longer he was out here, the more chance there was that he'd be a target.

Think, Ryan, think!

The colonel couldn't leave him out here all day, but he wouldn't let him back any time soon. And Ryan was desperate to get inside.

If he could just come up with something— *anything*—that would help the Forum solve the problem then the colonel might open the door.

He dropped on his butt, water soaking through his dirty shorts and boxers as he started doing sit-ups in the mud.

He was mad that the others had gotten him in this mess. It wasn't his fault that he was like the Outlier. So what if they both enjoyed hacking and came from privileged backgrounds? And was it any surprise that he didn't enjoy working in teams when people kept selling him out? No-one else from the Forum was being made to do sit-ups in the rain!

You're just like him.

Was it true? Not just superficially, but in a real, deep way? Was he destined to emerge from the academy as a bitter, twisted loner, hell-bent on revenge? He wouldn't say no to inflicting some pain and suffering on Colonel Keller.

The conditions were brutal. Rain hammered the back of his shirt as he dropped on to his front and forced his body up and down. Then, he started jogging down the pitch, knowing he was no closer to freedom.

The colonel had left Lee out here for an hour. And he hated Ryan even more. He could be here until lunchtime. Or longer.

Had the colonel done the same thing to the Outlier at some point? Had he punished him until the kid just couldn't take any more and snapped?

Ryan could see how that might happen.

He could see the colonel watching him through the classroom window. Was he smiling?

He suppressed the temptation to wave at him, to show him he couldn't be broken that easily. But deep inside, he wanted to cry. By the time he'd done another lap, his hands and feet were numb with cold.

You can do this, Ryan.

How was the Outlier hacking so many accounts at a time? Ryan hadn't been lying to the colonel: hacking into Lady Devonmoor's account would have taken days. And the work was mind-numbing and dull, not the fun, creative kind of hacking that Ryan enjoyed.

No-one would enjoy doing that. The idea of doing it again and again to one account after another was crazy. And sometimes just to move a hundred pounds. Or twenty. It didn't make sense.

There must be an easier way.

Something was bugging him, right at the back of his brain, but he was too tired to figure it out.

Back down on his butt. Another ten sit-ups. He was close to the trees. Any moment now he expected to see a red light staring back at him as the StealthBot emerged from the undergrowth. Should he and Sparks have told the staff about it? Were they being stupid keeping it secret?

No, Blackfell would be just like this. Running laps in the rain. Press-ups in the mud. But there it would happen every day, without end. They had to keep quiet.

And he had to keep running.

He had no choice.

The canteen bustled with people when Ryan showed up, dripping wet, and took his place in line.

Cadets stopped and stared as they caught sight of him shivering there, his kit drenched and smeared with mud, his hair plastered to his forehead. Ryan tried to ignore them. How he longed for his uniform right now, for the long grey trousers and the stiff jacket.

Lee left his table and wandered over. 'How long were you out there?'

'Since morning break.' Ryan coughed and spluttered like a dying man. He leaned against the wall. 'I'm sorry you got caught up in this.'

'Hey, it wasn't you. It was the colonel.' Lee looked him up and down. 'Besides, I didn't have it so bad. I could shower and change.'

'Don't worry. I can do that next Tuesday.' Ryan wiped his nose with his shirt. He didn't care what anyone thought.

'They can't make you keep wearing that?' Lee shook his head with disbelief. 'You'll die.'

'Tell that to the colonel.' Ryan sneezed. 'On second thoughts, don't. That's probably his plan. Don't worry. It'll soon dry now I'm back in the warm. I'll sit by myself. I know I smell like garbage.'

'You don't need to.' Lee glanced over his shoulder as he saw Sarrell approaching. 'Listen carefully. Six point two. Photons. Legionella. Henry the Fifth. AK-47.'

'What?' Ryan looked at Lee as if he'd gone mad.

But there was no time to explain. Sarrell was within earshot. 'Cadet Young, unless I'm very much mistaken, you have already received your lunch?'

'Yes, sir. I just wanted to check Ryan was ok. He didn't look so good.'

'I'm sure he's fine, aren't you, Jacobs?'

'Yeah. Sure.' Ryan started coughing again.

Sarrell laughed. 'He's just a little unfit. But I'm sure that by the end of this week, that will no longer be the case. Take your seat, cadet.'

Lee sat back down at the table next to Kev and Ayana, leaving Ryan alone with Sarrell.

'Want me to go and stick my head down a toilet?' Ryan looked up at the prefect, a hard look in his eyes. 'Or shall I start by tipping my lunch over my head?'

'We'll save those for another day.' Sarrell smirked at him. 'Right now, you're in such a state it wouldn't make much difference.'

He was right. It would be hard to make Ryan's condition any worse. But at least that meant Ryan could eat his lunch in peace. He just had to score high enough on the test to get decent food.

As he reached the terminal by the serving area, he realised what Lee had been talking about. The questions each day weren't random: every cadet was asked the same. And Lee had just given him the answers.

Six point two.
Photons.
Legionella.

115

Henry the Fifth.

AK-47.

He selected each of the answers in turn.

Lee had taken a risk. If you got caught cheating, you lived to regret it. But right now, Ryan could have kissed him. Five green ticks later, Ryan had a first-class lunch of sausage and mash with chocolate cake for dessert.

Ayana beckoned him over. 'You're sitting with us. We don't care if you smell. We usually cope, don't we?'

Ryan grinned. 'I guess. But is it usually this bad?'

He lifted his arm and leaned down towards her. She recoiled in disgust. 'If you do that again, I'm out of here.'

'I don't blame you.'

'Do you have to go back this afternoon? To the colonel?' Kev sounded worried. 'What do you think he'll do this time?'

Ryan shrugged. 'Something really terrible.'

'What could be worse than that?' Ayana wrinkled her nose.

'He might sing?' suggested Ryan.

The cadets burst out laughing.

'You're not afraid of him?' asked Jael in awe.

'A little,' admitted Ryan. 'But fear is his most powerful weapon. Without it, he's just a sad, power-crazed old man.'

Kev grinned at him. 'That might be true. But whatever you do, Ryan, NEVER let him hear you say that.'

21. TIRED

'You know more than you're letting on.' Dr Torren stared at him and Ryan fidgeted in the seat.

'No, sir. I'm just tired.'

'Don't lie to me, Ryan.'

'Honest, sir. I'm doing my best in the Forum. If I knew anything, I'd tell them.'

Ryan had been summoned to Dr Torren's office after lunch. He was surprised he was allowed to sit in one of the big leather chairs given the state he was in, but he was glad of the comfort after being on his legs all morning. He stared out of the window which overlooked the front garden of the academy. Thankfully, the woods were some distance away.

'The colonel has asked me to use any means necessary to find out what you know. So, if you don't tell me, you know what will happen?'

'You'll torture me?'

'Don't be silly.' Dr Torren was not impressed. He leaned back in his chair, narrowing his eyes. 'I don't need to resort to that.'

'The colonel did. He had me running laps out there.' Ryan thumbed towards the storm outside. 'Do you know how cold it is? And he still won't let me get changed.'

'That's because you cheated on a punishment run.' The teacher was immaculate as always, wearing a three-piece pin-stripe suit and a cravat. His goatee beard was trimmed to perfection. 'And then you didn't even change properly into your uniform as you left the gym. You're the only cadet I know who can't even do one punishment without earning another.'

'Apart from the Outlier,' blurted out Ryan. 'He was just like me, wasn't he?'

'Yes, Ryan, he was. There are uncanny similarities. But every person is unique.'

'Try telling the colonel that.'

'You think he's punishing you because you're like the Outlier?'

'For sure. That's why he hates me so much.'

'Possibly, but that's not what this is about.' Dr Torren sighed. 'You know, when the colonel told me he thought you knew something about the Outlier and his little scheme, I thought he was making it up. But now I'm inclined to think differently. I can see it in your eyes. You're hiding something.'

Yeah, a ten-ton killer robot.

Ryan glared at the teacher. 'I'm allowed secrets.'

'Not this time.' The doctor leaned forwards. 'The stakes are too high. If you don't tell me, Ryan, I have no choice but to hypnotise you.'

Ryan leaned forward and fiddled with the top of his football socks. He didn't want Dr Torren to see the fear on his face. 'I won't let you.'

The teacher laughed. 'Defiant to the end. You never disappoint, do you, Ryan? But more is at stake here than you realise. I'm afraid you don't have a choice.'

Ryan's heart was beating fast. He'd never been hypnotised, but from what he'd seen with other cadets, if Dr Torren put him into a trance then he'd sing like a canary. He'd blab all about the StealthBot, he'd grass up Sparks. It would all be over.

'Please don't.' Ryan looked up at the teacher. 'I'm begging you. Don't do it.'

Dr Torren stroked his beard, considering his request. 'It must be exhausting, Ryan, being this rebellious. You've already told me how tired you are. I don't imagine you got all that much sleep last night. You had to be up an hour early this morning, didn't you?'

'I barely slept,' muttered Ryan.

'And now you're here, in this warm room, sitting in a comfortable chair, completely safe...'

Until I get shot with a laser.

'Just lean back for a moment and close your eyes and think about it. What would make you happy right now? What would make this all go away? If you could make the decisions here, what would you change?'

The doctor's voice dripped into his brain like honey. Ryan knew he shouldn't listen: this was how it started. He couldn't let it happen. He wouldn't.

Don't let him do this!

'You're so relaxed in that chair, so safe, it would be a relief just to let go for a change…'

As the doctor spoke, Ryan thought about the opposite of whatever the doctor said. He was meant to be feeling warm and comfortable, so instead he imagined he was outside again, running laps in the torrential rain, frightened he'd get shot by the StealthBot. He remembered how the rain dripped from his hair and the way his cold, wet shorts stuck to his butt. He thought about the pain in his stomach every time he did another sit-up and how tired his legs felt. He shut out the doctor's voice, refusing to listen.

After a while, he realised that the doctor had stopped talking. Ryan remained still, his eyes closed.

'There we go,' said the doctor. 'That wasn't so hard, now, was it? Now let's see if we can finally uncover the truth.'

He thinks I'm in a trance.

If the doctor found out he wasn't, he'd try again. And next time, he might succeed. Ryan decided to play along.

'I'm going to ask you some questions, Ryan. And you just need to tell me the truth, ok?'

'Yes, sir.' Ryan said it as mechanically as he could.

'Excellent. Are you hiding something from us?'

Ryan wanted to say no, but Dr Torren was convinced he had a secret. He needed to give him something to throw him off the scent.

'Yes, sir.'

'What is it, Ryan?'

Think, Ryan, think.

He had to confess to something, else they'd find out about the robot. What would be bad enough to get him in serious trouble without alerting the doctor to the actual truth?

He spoke without emotion. 'I cheated again, sir. On the run this morning.'

Dr Torren laughed. 'You really are something else. How did you do that?'

'I took a shortcut on this side of the lake.'

'Let me get this straight. You did a run today as a punishment because you cheated on your run yesterday. And you cheated again?'

'Yes, sir.'

'Sergeant Wright is going to love this.'

Please don't tell him.

To his relief, the doctor changed the subject: 'What happened in the Forum the other day, just before the school was locked down?'

'I saw something aiming at Sarah Devonmoor.'

'Something?'

Ryan cursed inwardly as he realised he'd almost given the game away. He quickly covered his tracks. 'Some kind of weapon. I thought someone was about to kill her with it.'

The doctor stroked his goatee. 'And it was definitely pointing at Sarah?'

'Until I jumped on her.'

'I see.' The doctor changed subject again. 'Have you had any insights into how the Outlier is hacking bank accounts that you haven't shared?'

'No, sir.'

'No ideas at all?'

'No, sir.'

'Have you been giving the problem your full attention?'

'No, sir,' admitted Ryan.

'Well, Jacobs, from now on, that is going to change. Solving this problem is your number one priority. You will become obsessed with it. Every waking moment. When you are eating, you will think about it. When you are on the toilet, you'll try to solve it. When you are doing one of the many, many punishment runs that Sergeant Wright is going to make you do, you will still obsess about this problem. Until you solve it, it will be the driving motivation in your life. Do you understand?'

'Yes, sir.'

'In a moment I will count to three and click my fingers. You will wake up and you will remember nothing I have said to you while you have been asleep. However, when our meeting is over, you will insist on cleaning the chair you are sitting in.'

'Yes, sir.'

'One. Two. Three.' Dr Torren clicked his fingers.

Ryan opened his eyes and looked around, as if he were confused. 'What happened?'

'I hypnotised you, Ryan. See, that wasn't so bad?'

Ryan acted scared. 'Did I... did I tell you anything?'

'Nothing particularly useful. Though you might want to think about owning up to Sergeant Wright about your little shortcut before I get a chance to tell him myself.'

Ryan leaned forward, his head in his hands. 'I said that?'

'Of course.'

'If he finds out I cheated again, he'll destroy me.'

'And you deserve it, Ryan. I've never known anyone who cheats so much. You clearly haven't learned your lesson.'

'I suppose. Can I go now, sir? I need to get back to the Forum.'

Dr Torren smiled. 'Feel free. I'm glad we had this little chat.'

As Ryan stood up, he glanced down at the seat. Mud was smeared over the soft leather. 'First, I'll get a cloth and clean your chair, sir. I didn't mean to mess it up.'

'If you insist, Ryan.'

As Ryan headed to the cleaning store, he shuddered as he realised how close he had come to being hypnotised. But he'd managed to stay in control. It had taken a lot of effort, but he'd stopped Dr Torren messing with his brain, this time at least. That had to be a good sign.

One way or another, the teachers at Devonmoor were determined to get him under control.

And he was just as determined to resist.

***

The corridor around the corner from the staff room was deserted. Most of the students and teachers were in lessons, but Ryan could hear someone approaching, so he slipped inside the cleaning cupboard and waited in case it was Sarrell or Sergeant Wright.

He needn't have worried. He recognised the first voice straight away; it was Mr Davids.

But who was with him? As Ryan strained his ears, he realised it was Mr McAllister, the genius inventor who taught engineering at Devonmoor. They were two of the nicest teachers at the academy.

But their hushed tones made Ryan curious. He listened carefully, trying to eavesdrop through the thin door.

'I know what you're saying, Lionel,' said Mr McAllister. 'But we can't allow the Outlier to have the Fractal Processor. It's too powerful. We agreed that we would keep it here. Even the Ministry of Defence can't be trusted with something like that. We can hardly give it to a rebel like him.'

Mr Davids didn't seem so sure. 'I don't think he'd do anything terrible with it. He's not like that. He just wants it for one of his projects.'

'Like stealing Lady Devonmoor's fortune? And hacking thousands of bank accounts? You give that boy too much credit, Lionel. He tried to have Sarah Devonmoor killed!'

Mr Davids sighed. 'It just doesn't seem like something he'd do.'

'Either way, if we don't solve this conundrum soon, there won't even be a school. He's already taken half the Devonmoor fortune…'

The teachers continued their quiet conversation, but they were too far away for Ryan to hear.

So, that's what the Outlier really wanted. He was after some invention that was kept here at the school. Something powerful and dangerous.

And unless the Forum could work out how he was stealing all the money, he could eventually succeed.

Whatever it took, they needed to stop him.

Before it was too late.

22. ERROR

The afternoon dragged. The colonel was frustrated at the lack of progress in the Forum and the cadets were getting bored with the problem.

'Today's performance has been unacceptable,' hissed the colonel, as they stood to attention in his classroom at the end of the session. 'You're all an embarrassment to this academy. You will go away and think on your performance. Tomorrow, you will return here and each of you will present a working theory on how the Outlier has accomplished this seemingly impossible feat. Anyone who fails to do so will be punished. Dismissed.'

The cadets filed miserably from the room.

'What does he want from us?' one cadet murmured. 'We've already discussed every possibility. We can't invent new ones from thin air.'

'We're screwed,' agreed another.

'You have to solve this, Ryan,' muttered Jael. 'You know more about this than anyone.'

'He's right,' said Ranjit. 'You need to get the colonel off our back.'

'If I could, I would, ok?' snapped back Ryan. 'Do you think I spent hours doing laps just for fun? Or I enjoyed watching Lee freezing to death out there?'

Ranjit shrugged. 'I guess not.'

'Then lay off!'

Sparks put a hand on Ryan's shoulder, pulling him aside. 'You ready?' he asked. 'I thought we might head straight to engineering.'

Ryan looked around at the dispersing cadets. Several of them were giving him evil looks: *This is all your fault.*

'Sounds good to me.'

As they opened the door to the warehouse, Sparks shielded his face from the rain. 'We're gonna get drenched.'

'Yeah, well I'm used to that.' Ryan pulled on his trainers. 'Imagine having to run laps in it for two hours.'

Sparks gave him an apologetic look. 'The colonel is so harsh.'

'You wait until Sergeant Wright finds out I cheated on my run this morning. He may do something worse.'

'You're gonna tell him?'

'I have to, or Dr Torren will.'

They dashed towards the warehouse.

'So, how do we capture this thing?' asked Ryan.

'I'm going to cross-wire the cables to the plug point. The moment the StealthBot plugs itself in, it'll get ten thousand volts running through it.'

'And that'll knock it out?'

'Yeah, should do,' said Sparks, over the sounds of the wind. 'If not, it's gonna be pretty hacked off. But with any luck, the electricity will short-circuit its battery. Then we just have to get the central processing unit unplugged. Without that, it's just an enormous heap of metal.'

They arrived at the warehouse door and slipped inside.

'Wait, rewind a second. You mean, we might just make it mad?'

'It's possible,' replied Sparks.

Ryan shook the water out of his hair. 'And that doesn't worry you? Having a killer robot with the mother of all headaches?'

'Of course it worries me, Ryan.' Sparks looked up at him with tired eyes. 'This all worries me. But I'm doing my best, ok? Besides, the power surge will trip the switch on the circuit. Once that's happened, there will be no power anywhere in engineering. So, the worst that will happen is we have to wait for the StealthBot to run out of power.'

'How long would that take?'

'One hour. Maybe two. It can't have much left. The lasers use a lot. Anyway, I have to go and switch off the power so I can rewire the circuit.'

'Knock yourself out,' said Ryan. Then he grinned at Sparks. 'Not literally, of course.'

His friend gave a weak smile. 'I'll try not to.' He headed to the far corner. 'The trip-switches are somewhere over here.'

'And you reckon the robot is gonna arrive in an hour?' Ryan called over to him.

'Yeah, we should have plenty of time.'

They were fatal last words. There was a colossal bang as the door to the warehouse was flung open. Heavy metal footsteps echoed off the corrugated tin walls. Sparks was behind a bank of machines, well out of sight, but Ryan was in the centre of the room as the StealthBot strode in.

Don't move, Ryan.

He remembered what Sparks had said about movement being the primary way the robot identified a threat. He stood still, like he was being inspected by the colonel.

The robot scanned the room.

'POWER SOURCE IDENTIFIED.'

The metallic voice sent a shiver down Ryan's spine. That thing could cut him in two with a wave of its arm. He hoped it would walk over to the far corner, well away from where he stood.

He wasn't that lucky.

The robot moved directly in front of him. It held up one of its arms. With a sudden movement, it stuck three metal prongs in the power outlet on the wall. There was no sudden power surge or shower of sparks. The robot twisted around to survey the room, in a manouevre that would have broken a human arm.

'SURVEILLANCE MODE ENGAGED.'

It stood only a few metres away, its red eye glowing. It was watching him. If he moved, even a centimetre, it would identify him as a threat. And then it would use its other arm—the one with the laser—to slice him up.

It was cold in the warehouse and Ryan's kit was damp. It was hard not to shiver. As he stood there, he wondered if Sparks was also frozen to the spot.

It won't be for long.

That's what Sparks had said. But that was when he thought he'd have time to enact his plan. If the power hadn't been turned off, then the StealthBot wouldn't run out of battery at all. It would stay there until it was fully charged. Would that only take an hour? Or would it take all night?

The red eye stared at him, daring him to move.

But if he did, he would die.

Come on!

Ryan breathed slowly, afraid that any slight movement might trigger the robot's motion sensor.

He considered making a break for it, and sprinting for the door, but he knew how quickly the robot could react. That would be suicide.

He waited.

Ryan had the grim realisation that he needed to pee. He should have gone to the toilet as soon as he left the Forum, but he'd planned to use the one in the warehouse. Now, that wasn't possible and he was busting to go.

Minutes ticked by.

He tried to take his mind off his discomfort by thinking about the Outlier and how he was hacking the bank accounts. He'd almost had a breakthrough earlier, but it had slipped from his grasp, the same way a dream dissolves the moment you wake. They were missing something, and deep in his unconscious, he knew what it was.

What was Sparks doing?

If the colonel was right about pain helping you focus, then he'd approve of Ryan's current situation. Even in drill, he didn't have to stand for this length of time.

It was no good. He couldn't hold it any longer. He felt the pee soaking his boxers and shorts before running down his leg to his football socks.

Great. As if the kit didn't smell bad enough already. But, right now, it was hard to be worried about that.

He stared at the StealthBot. If he hadn't given it free-will in the first place, none of this would have happened. All of this was his own stupid fault.

His legs were tired and he wasn't sure how much longer he'd be able to stay in this position.

He'd already lost track of time. It was the most surreal staring contest in history. And unless Sparks got a move on, Ryan was doomed to lose.

Come on, Sparks.

***

Ryan had almost given up when the lights went out without warning.

Complete, utter darkness, except for the red glow of the StealthBot's eye.

What was happening now?

A loud bang, followed by a flash of light and a shower of sparks, like someone had set a firework off in his face.

He reacted without thinking, shielding his eyes.

'THREAT DETECTED.'

'Run, Ryan, run!' Sparks was shouting from somewhere across the warehouse.

Ryan sprinted towards the door, but couldn't see. He slammed painfully into a workbench in the darkness, which sent him sprawling.

Lights flickered on and off as he scrambled behind a large metal storage unit. The StealthBot was jerking around, its arms and legs flying in random directions. It looked angry.

'Sparks, I need some help here!' Ryan hugged his legs, the smell of stale urine filling his nostrils.

This was some way to die.

The storage unit went flying, nuts, bolts and screws scattering across the warehouse floor.

The StealthBot bore down on him. Ryan kicked out, but his foot was no match for the shiny black armour plating.

'SPARKS! I'M GONNA DIE!'

It lifted its laser.

'THREAT DETECTED.'

Ryan looked up into the red eye, knowing it was the last thing he'd ever see.

23. SCREWS

Another explosion.

Instead of firing, the robot toppled forward. Ryan rolled to the side as it crashed down, missing him by millimetres.

It twitched, its pincers grabbing hold of his ankle in a last sudden movement. Ryan thought for a moment it would rip his foot off. He couldn't get away.

'THREAT DETECTED.'

The robot was dragging him towards its prostrate body, as if it planned to eat him.

Sparks ran over, a smoking weapon in his hands. He jumped on the robot's back and reached up the back of its neck. A second later the thing went limp, but it didn't release Ryan's foot.

'Are you trying to kill me?' shouted Ryan. 'It almost crushed me to death!'

Sparks looked embarrassed. 'Sorry. I didn't know what else to do. I didn't expect you to be lying there.'

'Neither did I.' Ryan nudged the robot's head with his other foot. 'Is it dead?'

'Disabled, yes. Pretty badly damaged, poor thing.'

'*Poor thing?* It shot at me!'

'It was just defending itself.'

'You're nuts.' Ryan gave a weak smile as he realised their ordeal was over. 'We did it, though, Sparks. We've captured the StealthBot. No-one ever needs to know.'

'Well, before you get too excited, let's get it hidden. Are you gonna get up or what?'

'It still has me by the ankle.'

'Oh.'

Sparks examined the pincers and fetched a toolbox. Two minutes later, Ryan's foot was free.

The two boys grabbed a machine trolley. With a lot of pulling and grunting, they dragged and rolled the robot's carcass on to it. Then they wheeled it to the far corner of the warehouse.

'I'm not sure we should ever turn this thing on again.' Ryan said, wiping sweat from his forehead. 'It's too dangerous. It could kill someone.'

'It wouldn't be a very effective military robot if it didn't,' Sparks pointed out.

'I know, but still.'

'We don't have to decide right now. Let's just get this mess cleared up and get to the canteen. It's nearly time for dinner.'

They pushed the StealthBot behind some steel panels and hid it under some sheets, then hauled the storage unit upright.

'You're sure it won't switch itself back on?' asked Ryan, glancing over to the far corner.

'I'm sure. I took this out.' Sparks held up a circuit board. 'I don't think it will be able to do much damage without a brain.'

'I dunno,' said Ryan, grinning. 'Sarrell manages to.'

The smile fell from his face the moment he turned around. Sarrell was standing right behind him and he did not look happy.

'Want to say that again, Jacobs?'

Ryan gulped. 'No.'

'What exactly has been happening here?' Sarrell gestured towards the warehouse floor which was covered in thousands of nuts, bolts and screws.

'It was my fault,' said Ryan, stalling for time. 'I, er, was trying out one of Sparks' new weapons without his permission. It went wrong and knocked the storage unit over.'

Sarrell smirked at him. 'Well, in that case Jacobs, I think you have some cleaning up to do.'

'Yeah, I know. We'll start straight after dinner.'

'No, Jacobs, you'll do it now. By yourself. You're not going to leave this warehouse until every single screw is back where it belongs.'

'But that'll take hours!'

Sarrell gave a wicked grin. 'What's your point?'

Ryan groaned and dropped to his knees on the cold concrete floor.

Sarrell kicked some screws, sending them flying. 'Don't get them mixed up now, will you? I will check. And if I find you have put any in the wrong place, then I'll empty them back out and you can start again.'

Ryan looked at the tiny pieces of metal, scattered over the floor.

'Cadet Sparks. Go to the canteen. And don't come back. Jacobs can do this alone.'

Sparks gave Ryan an apologetic look and hurried off to get his dinner.

Ryan started work. Every nut and screw was a different length. He had to measure and compare them before putting them in the compartments.

Sarrell sat down on a stool, resting his heavy boots on a workbench. 'I know you must hate me now, Jacobs, but in a few years time you'll thank me for toughening you up.'

'Yeah, sure.'

Like hell I will.

The older cadet stood up. 'I'm off to get some food. Who knows, I might bring you something back, but I wouldn't hold my breath if I were you.' Sarrell laughed at his own joke. 'Don't go anywhere.'

Ryan considered following the prefect out of the warehouse and seeing whether he could at least sneak some food before coming back. But that would be asking for trouble. And even by his standards, he was in enough of that as it was.

So, instead, he just got on with the long task of cleaning up the warehouse.

Picking up the screws was painstaking work: bending down, getting another handful of stuff, sorting through it, putting each piece in the right compartment. He wondered if some people did this kind of thing in factories. He'd never cope.

But then, in a way, it reminded him of hacking. Sorting through data, piece by piece, comparing and storing everything carefully. That's why the problem with the Outlier made no sense. Cracking passwords was like this; work he'd never enjoy. Which meant the Outlier would hate doing it too.

Breaking into that many bank accounts would be like knocking over a hundred of those storage units and then having to sort out the screws one by one, all by yourself, with no help.

How was the Outlier doing it?

It was no good. He was too tired to focus. It took all his brainpower to sort the screws.

Over two hours later, Sarrell returned. 'Still at it, Jacobs?'

'I'm nearly done.' Ryan glanced around. Most of the screws were back in their compartments.

Sarrell stood over him and sniffed the air. 'That smell is coming from you, isn't it? Have you wet yourself? Again?'

'No,' lied Ryan. He tried to crawl away, but Sarrell bent down and sniffed again.

'You have. How old are you, Jacobs?'

'Thirteen,' muttered Ryan.

'And you still wet yourself. This isn't even the first time!'

That was true. Ryan had an accident when he was doing the assault course at Devonmoor, which everyone knew about. Then there was the time he'd been locked in a cage.

'And you're going to wear that kit all week?'

Ryan grunted. Now that he no longer faced imminent death, the terrible reality of what that was going to be like began to sink in. His shorts and socks were grim. 'So, what happens now? Got any more fun games for me this evening? You know, to toughen me up?' He knew it was a dangerous thing to say, but he was too angry to stay quiet.

'That's one thing I like about you, Jacobs. You have spirit. I'll give you that.' Sarrell checked the clock on the wall. 'But it's not long until lights out so I'll just let you finish up here tonight. We can always play some more later in the week.'

The threat in Sarrell's voice was unmistakable.

Ryan was already having the worst week of his life.

And it was only going to get worse.

24. SHOWER

The dormitory was empty when Ryan arrived. There was still half an hour until lights out. The other boys would be in the common room, having fun. Ryan could barely remember what that was like; he just seemed to ricochet from one punishment to another.

Get a grip, Ryan.

He looked towards the bathroom, then glanced down at his filthy kit. An idea formed in his mind. He was already for it in the morning. Sergeant Wright would tear into him as soon as he found out that Ryan had cheated on his run. He was going to spend the next few days being punished. So, what difference did it make if he took a shower? Besides, if he was clever, no-one would know.

He stripped off his clothes and stepped under the hot water. He couldn't get clean fast enough. The shampoo felt amazing in his hair, washing away the remains of the stew. He didn't dare to use shower gel in case the smell gave him away; he was just content to wash away the sweat and dirt.

It felt so good.

After he'd stood there as long as he dared, he stepped out, drying himself double-quick.

To his surprise, Lee was sitting on his bunk. The blond boy looked up in surprise as Ryan exited the bathroom.

'Ryan, you didn't!' Lee was horrified. If Ryan got caught, the whole dorm would pay.

'Don't worry. I've got a plan.' Ryan reached down into the laundry basket and rummaged around. He pulled out Lee's muddy sports kit. 'Mind if I borrow this?'

Lee shrugged. 'Sure. But even I wouldn't go anywhere near that. You must be desperate.'

'I am.' Ryan tugged it on.

'Mate, that's rank.' Lee grimaced as Ryan pulled on the dirty socks.

'Not as rank as mine. You only wore this for a couple of hours. What's a bit of mud and sweat between friends?'

'You're insane.' Lee couldn't help grinning. 'What's the point of having a shower and then putting on a dirty kit?'

'Because it's not the mud that's the problem. It's the smell. My old kit stank. Want a sniff?' Ryan picked up his rugby shirt from the floor and held it out to his friend.

'I'll pass,' smiled Lee. 'I can smell it from here.'

'Well, compared to that, your stale sweat is like expensive after-shave. But I'm hoping that it will still be enough to convince Sergeant Wright that I haven't changed.' Ryan threw his old kit into the laundry and put the lid back.

'But what about your legs and face. They're way too clean.'

'They never said I wasn't allowed to wash those. Besides, the rain washed most of the mud off even before I got in the shower.'

'Reckon you'll get away with it?' Lee propped himself up on an elbow. 'If you get busted again, I don't even wanna know what's gonna happen.'

'Me neither,' admitted Ryan. 'Dr Torren is already making me confess I cheated on the run.'

Lee groaned. 'You're kidding? You cheated *again*? Are you mental?'

Ryan jumped into bed. 'The trick with punishments, Lee, is to get so many that they just can't get worse.'

'Or you could just not get any? Have you thought of that?'

Ryan looked over at him. 'You know me. That's never gonna happen.'

Lee smiled. 'True.' Then, after a moment, he thought of something else. 'Speaking of punishments, I don't suppose you've solved the puzzle yet, for the Forum?'

'Not yet,' admitted Ryan.

'Neither has anyone else,' said Lee, miserably. 'We're all doomed.'

***

Ryan slid his feet down the corridor and knocked on Sergeant Wright's door. With the StealthBot captured, he'd slept well; it was just a shame he still had to get up an hour before everyone else.

'Morning, Jacobs.'

The sergeant didn't seem too angry; he hadn't heard anything from Dr Torren yet. But there was nothing to gain by keeping him waiting.

'I need to tell you something, sir. And you're not gonna like it.'

'I see.' Sergeant Wright walked back to his desk and perched himself on the edge. 'Well, go on. Don't leave me in suspense.'

'I didn't do the full run yesterday. I stayed this side of the lake and took a shortcut.'

'What? How?' Sergeant Wright looked perplexed. 'There's a fence.'

'There's a hole in it.' Ryan decided not to explain how that got there.

'And why did you decide to take a shortcut, Jacobs?'

'You know why, sir.' Ryan shrugged. 'I'm lazy, cheating scum, remember?'

'I think you forgot the second part,' pointed out the sergeant.

'And I deserve to be punished,' muttered Ryan.

'You do, Jacobs. And you will be. But I'm still a little confused. Why are you telling me this now?'

There was no point hiding it. 'Dr Torren found out. He told me I had to tell you.'

Sergeant Wright laughed. 'And here I was thinking you'd had a sudden pang of guilt and decided to come clean! But even now you're only telling me because you have to.'

'I guess.'

Yeah, I can't do anything right.

'Wait for me in the gym.'

Ryan stood in the sports hall, wondering what would happen. Even longer in the kit? Maybe. Extra runs? Probably. But it wasn't enough. He knew it and the sergeant knew it. That's what scared him.

He felt like he'd crossed a line. Cheating in a lesson was bad. Doing it in detention was suicide. And he'd now done it twice. Even he couldn't keep track of how many rules he'd broken. The sergeant didn't know the half of it.

When the teacher entered the room, he walked slowly across the hall, each footstep a nail in Ryan's coffin. 'Hold out your hand.'

The sergeant took hold of Ryan's wrist and fastened some kind of band around it, fiddling for a while with the clip. 'This is a tag. It will track you at all times in your movements around the academy. It also acts as a fitness band, tracking your speed and heart-rate.'

'So I don't cheat?'

'Exactly, Jacobs. From now on, taking short cuts is not an option.'

'Why didn't you make me wear one before?'

'Because cadets rarely cheat at Devonmoor.' Sergeant Wright started pacing up and down the room. 'In fact, Jacobs, I've never known anyone like you. I don't see why I should have to invent additional punishments just because you keep breaking the rules.'

'You're not going to punish me?'

'Oh, I am. But *I'm* not going to come up with the punishment. *You* are. Tonight, you will write down the worst punishment you can think of—something that even you would be afraid of doing. It has to be worse than anything you or any other cadet has done before.'

Ryan gulped. 'And if I don't?'

'Classic, Jacobs. Only you would ask that question. If you don't, or if the punishment you come up with is not terrible, then every lad in your dormitory will suffer. Do you want that to happen?'

'No, sir.'

'I'm looking forward to seeing your ideas. We're going to teach you not to cheat, Jacobs. By fair means or foul.'

'Yes, sir.'

'I think you'd better make a start on that run, don't you?'

25. BREAKTHROUGH

Ryan arrived in the canteen dripping with sweat. He'd only just made it in time for breakfast.

'Still smelling like a toilet, Jacobs?' Sarrell was on duty and sneered at him as he took his place in line.

'I guess.' Ryan looked away. He didn't want a fight.

With Sarrell watching him like a hawk, Lee didn't dare sneak up and give him the answers so Ryan struggled his way through the canteen test, only scoring three out of five. After missing dinner the previous night, he was longing for a cooked breakfast, but that wasn't going to happen. He had to settle for porridge and fruit.

'How was it?' asked Lee, as he took his seat. 'I'm surprised you're allowed to eat.'

'Me too,' admitted Ryan. 'But it's bad. I have to design my own punishment. Something more severe than anything anyone's thought of before.'

'You're not serious?' Kev almost choked on his toast.

'But can't you just come up with something mild?' pointed out Jael. 'What happens if you do that?'

'Trust me,' said Ryan, 'you boys don't want to know.'

As the conversation turned to more cheerful matters, Ryan found it hard to take his mind off the problem facing the Forum. He'd been so close to cracking it. The answer was there, flirting with his consciousness. If only he could somehow get hold of it.

I am lazy, cheating scum and I deserve to be punished.

There it was again. Every time he thought about those words, it came closer. As if the answer lay there, right at the heart of the sentence.

What was his brain trying to tell him? He was lazy. He knew that, if he was honest. And he was a cheat. Even he couldn't deny it. Did he deserve to be punished? Probably. That didn't mean he had to enjoy it.

So, why was it bothering him so much?

In some ways Sergeant Wright had a nerve, calling him lazy when he couldn't be bothered to think up a punishment himself. It was a bit like copying someone else's homework; making someone else put all the effort instead.

Yes, that was it.

And again, there it was.

A glimpse of the answer.

Jumping up from the table, he almost knocked over Jael's drink.

'Hey, watch out!'

'Sorry,' Ryan backed away. 'There's someone I need to see. I'll catch you guys later.'

Leaving a trail of confusion in his wake, Ryan ran out of the canteen and dashed down the corridor to the oldest part of the school.

***

She was there, in her office.

Sat on an armchair, drinking tea.

The door was ajar, as if she were expecting a visitor.

Ryan knocked gently and peered through the gap. 'Lady Devonmoor? May I speak with you a moment?'

She looked up, surprised to see him. 'Ryan, dear. Do come in. How lovely to see you.'

He wandered over and stood awkwardly beside a floral sofa by the enormous bay window. He didn't want to get these seats dirty. It didn't seem fair.

'Isn't it a bit early for football?'

Ryan looked down at his muddy kit. 'Oh, I had to do a run this morning. And I'm not allowed to change. It's a long story.'

'I see.' Lady Devonmoor gestured towards the table. 'Would you like a spot of tea?'

'No thanks, ma'am.' Ryan was keen to get to the point. 'I just need to ask you a question. It's about the Outlier, and the problem we're trying to solve in the Forum.'

'Ah, yes. A very tricky issue indeed. Sam is being totally unreasonable. Such a clever boy, but so bitter. So misunderstood. What do you want to know?'

'It's something about your finances.' Ryan fidgeted a little, rubbing one foot with the other. 'If it's not too nosey to ask, I mean, if you don't mind saying, I wondered if you've made any new investments recently?'

'New investments?' The old lady looked for a moment out of the window, rubbing her chin. 'Yes, I think we made one or two in the last six months. That's not unusual, of course.'

'Did you set up a new account with any of them?' Ryan was desperate to get to the truth.

'Well, yes, I did. A company called Kurio Holdings. But we didn't invest much. And before you ask, that's not the account that money went missing from, so I don't imagine it's much help.'

'It might be, ma'am. Thank you.' Ryan backed out of the office, almost bumping into Dr Torren.

'Sorry, sir, I didn't see you there.'

'Having any luck with our little puzzle, Jacobs?'

'I think I am! I'll tell you later, sir.'

As soon as he was out of the teacher's sight, Ryan dashed off down the corridor.

***

He burst through the door to Colonel Keller's classroom. The room was empty, even though it was almost time for the session to start.

Where could they be?

He turned back around, hoping to intercept some stragglers in the canteen.

As he hurtled around the corner, he ran straight into Sarrell, who grabbed hold of his shirt.

'In a hurry, Jacobs?'

'I'm meant to be at the Forum, but no-one is in the classroom. I don't know where they all are.'

'Ah yes, you missed drill again, didn't you?'

'It's not my fault. I was doing a run. Where are they?'

'They're over at the assault course. If I were you, I'd get a move on. The colonel looked pretty angry when he gave the notice.' Sarrell pushed Ryan away, making him stumble.

'Thanks, I guess.'

It wasn't the news he wanted to hear. The assault course was miles away. He guessed the colonel was planning to use it in some creative way to motivate them. But once he'd heard what Ryan had to say, he'd hopefully change his mind.

Ryan set off across the sports field and back into the woods, his legs already aching from his long run before breakfast. He'd never done so much exercise in his life.

But fifteen minutes later, he arrived to find the place deserted. Tyres hung on ropes above muddy ditches, swaying in the wind. A crawl net lay on the ground, submerged in mud. But there were no cadets.

Sarrell had lied. Not only had he made Ryan run an extra few miles, he'd also ensured that Ryan arrived at the Forum stupidly late. Ryan would face the full force of the colonel's wrath. He groaned and started back, forcing his legs to go as fast as they could.

More mud.

More sweat.

More pain.

And the only thing Ryan had to look forward to was another long day at Devonmoor.

26. LAZY

'Well, look who it is.' Sarcasm dripped from the colonel's voice. 'Thank you so much for joining us, Jacobs. I'm sure you have much better things to do than to be here.'

'I'm sorry, sir. I didn't know where we were meeting.' Ryan walked in to the circular room at the top of the academy. The windows had been fixed so there was no need for the Forum to meet anywhere else.

'And it took you over half an hour to find us?' The colonel tilted his head. 'You expect me to believe that? Aren't you meant to be a genius?'

'I thought you were at the assault course.'

'Whatever gave you that idea?'

Sarrell.

But he couldn't say that. It would only make things worse if the older cadet found out he'd told.

'I don't know, sir.'

'You don't know.'

'No. But just listen! I've had a breakthrough! I think I know how the Outlier did it!'

The colonel's expression changed. He sat down on a stool at the front of the room and beckoned Ryan forward. 'Let's hear it, Jacobs. But I hope you're not making this up to distract me from your tardiness. Or our next session *will* be at the assault course.'

Ryan remembered the time he'd had to complete the course while handcuffed to Sarrell and Drew. He shuddered. He hoped the colonel liked what he was about to say.

'You were right,' he said, looking around at the students. 'All of you. I'm just like the Outlier. We have loads in common. I just didn't want to admit it. And you were also right, Colonel, you and Sergeant Wright.'

The colonel stood, arms folded. His eyes narrowed: *Get on with it, Jacobs.*

'I'm lazy, cheating scum. Every time I get given work, I try to avoid it. Whenever I get punished, I find a way to cheat. And we know from the Outlier's records, he was just like that. Always getting away with stuff, always pulling the wool over people's eyes.'

'So?' Sarah wasn't impressed. They'd heard all this before.

'So, there's no way that the Outlier would spend hours hacking into all these bank accounts, cracking passwords and analysing PIN codes. He'd hate it. It's like doing hours of maths homework. He'd find an easier way. So, I got thinking: how would I do it? What's the shortcut?'

The colonel tutted, as if disgusted by Ryan's desire to avoid work, but he didn't interrupt.

'I'd get them all to give me their passwords and their PIN numbers. And their sort codes and account numbers while they were at it. Then I wouldn't need to crack anything.'

'But they're hardly going to hand those kinds of sensitive details over,' pointed out Ranjit. 'It's hard work to get people to disclose something like that, even for a con artist.'

'You'd think.' Ryan wished the colonel would let him sit down. He felt awkward standing in the middle of the room, and his legs ached. 'But here's what he did. He set up a fake company called "Kurio Holdings". He marketed it to the super-rich as a great option for investments. Over time, rich people set up accounts, Lady Devonmoor included.'

'It doesn't solve the problem,' objected Sarah. 'The money went missing from different banks. And I don't think that was one of them.'

'It wasn't,' agreed Ryan. 'But he didn't want to keep the money they invested in his fake company. He simply needed them to set up an account.'

The cadets looked blank. They had no idea what he was talking about. He pressed on, a sense of urgency in his voice: 'All of you will have loads of online accounts for stuff, right? I mean, you have your login for the school network, there's stuff you use on the Internet, when you access social media during the holidays. All of those things need passwords. Ever used the same password more than once?'

Ryan looked around. A few of the cadets nodded. Others looked at the floor.

'We all do it! Partly because we can't remember them if they're different. And partly because it's hard to think of new ones all the time. Creating stuff from scratch is hard work. We all have our little mental ruts. There are passwords we use and re-use. When people sign up for an account with Kurio Holdings, they choose a password and a PIN, and memorable questions, just as you do with any other account. But what people don't realise is that the Outlier then uses those same details to access their accounts at other banks.'

'Would that work?' Sarah didn't look convinced. 'People aren't that stupid.'

'They are. You are. Even I am, and I'm a hacker. We all do it. And it did work. That's how he pulled this whole thing off. He didn't need to crack a single password. He just had to get people to give them to him.'

Jael had a look of intense concentration on his face. 'But he moved the money through normal accounts too. A lot of those people wouldn't use an investment broker.'

'No, that's true. But he could have done exactly the same thing using a different honey-trap. Maybe they fancied some bitcoin. Or liked a flutter on a gambling site. I don't know what he used, but if we can look through the account transactions, we just have to find one or two sites they are all connected to. It doesn't matter if they transferred much money or not, as long as they set up an account.'

'It sounds possible,' said Jael. 'I think you might be on to something.'

'I think so too,' agreed Yu. 'It's the only way he could have done it. That's brilliant, Ryan.'

Ryan smiled. 'Thanks. Seems that being lazy has some advantages, after all.'

'But how did he get the money back to his own account at the end of it all?' Sarah glared at him, annoyed.

'I still haven't worked that out,' admitted Ryan. 'But if the evidence backs up what I'm saying, we can at least stop him taking any more.'

'In that case, get to it!' barked the colonel. 'Look into everything that Jacobs has said. If he's right, then we need to alert Lady Devonmoor and the other investors so they can secure their accounts. If he's wrong...' He paused and looked at Ryan. 'Well, if he's wrong then he's going to be very sorry indeed.'

Ryan swallowed. 'I'm right, sir. You'll see.'

'We will, Jacobs.' The colonel clapped his hands, and the cadets got to work, the Forum becoming a hive of activity.

'Cadet Young,' called the colonel. 'Fetch Mr Davids, Dr Fleur and Lady Devonmoor. Tell them we've got a lead and we need them up here.'

'Yes, sir.' Lee saluted and headed off.

Within minutes, the staff had arrived. Ryan explained his theory to them while the other cadets beavered away.

'Of course!' Mr Davids smacked himself on the head, frustrated he hadn't thought of it. 'I've spent the last few days trying to create a program that can hack thousands of bank accounts at the same time—the hacker's holy grail. It's almost driven me mad! I couldn't work out how he'd done it. But that's because he didn't. He didn't need anything that complex!'

'I feel so foolish,' muttered Lady Devonmoor. 'Using the same password. What a stupid old lady I've become.'

'Just change your details now,' urged Ryan. 'Every account you have. New passwords and PIN numbers. They all need to be different.'

'I will.' Lady Devonmoor stood up. 'I'll do it immediately.'

'That's not the only thing that needs to get changed around here,' said Dr Fleur, her nose wrinkling. 'Just how long have you been wearing that kit?'

'A few days,' admitted Ryan. 'It's a punishment.'

'For us or for you?'

Ryan smiled. 'You'll need to ask the colonel.'

'You've done a good job, Ryan, my boy.' Mr Davids clapped him on the back. 'It's an old scam, almost too old. I thought someone as clever as the Outlier would do something much more complicated.'

'So did I. Then I realised he wouldn't go to that amount of effort. Not if he's as lazy as me. He'd keep it simple and just cheat everyone out of their passwords.'

'Well, let's see if this all checks out.' Dr Fleur took a place at one of the computers around the edge of the room and Mr Davids sat down at the one next to her.

With the teachers aiding the effort, it didn't take long to uncover the truth. Ryan was right. Not only had Kurio Holdings been set up as a fake investment company, but some smaller puzzle and competition websites had been used as well, drawing in people from across the social spectrum.

Ryan flinched as the colonel put his hand on Ryan's shoulder.

'As you've solved the mystery, I am going to reward you by not punishing you for turning up late this morning.'

Really? That's my reward?

'Thanks, sir.' Ryan knew better than to complain.

'However, I hear you cheated on the run again yesterday.' The colonel's grip tightened.

'Yes, sir. Sergeant Wright is making me come up with my own punishment.'

That had been the last piece of the puzzle. Ryan had been thinking about the implications of the Outlier being lazy for some time. But the breakthrough came when he realised that even someone as disciplined and motivated as Sergeant Wright was too lazy to think up a new punishment for him. He'd got to thinking about that, and something clicked into place: *I bet Sergeant Wright is the kind of person who uses the same passwords for everything.*

That was when he knew just how the Outlier had done it. He thought about explaining that to the colonel, but looking into that stern face, he knew he'd be wasting his breath.

'This doesn't change anything, Jacobs.' The colonel drawled it, as if savouring the words. 'Your brief moment of triumph in the Forum doesn't change the fact that you have repeatedly cheated your way out of one punishment after another.'

'No, sir.'

'I will join you and Sergeant Wright tomorrow morning. I look forward to seeing what you have come up with as a suitable punishment for your actions. It had better be severe, or you know what will happen.'

'Yes, sir.'

He couldn't let them drag Lee, Kev and Jael down with him. He needed to play along.

The colonel let go of his shoulder. 'One day, Jacobs, you will look back at these days and realise the benefits of discipline. You will be thankful for all you learned at Devonmoor.'

Ryan couldn't let that go unchallenged. 'But I won't! You say I'm just like the Outlier. Well, he's not thankful, is he? You punished him so much, he hates this school and everything it stands for.'

'That just shows how little you know, Jacobs.' The colonel looked away. 'I would have broken the Outlier, given half a chance. But others interfered. They thought it would be best if we took a softer approach, so we laid off him in the end. And look where that got us. He still thought he was treated unfairly, of course, even though he was saved from the worst of it. He was a weak and snivelling little brat, spoilt just like you. He could never accept when he was wrong. But believe me: this time, I won't make the same mistake. I don't intend to leave the job half-finished. By the time you're done here, you will have learned to respect authority. You hear me?'

'I guess so, sir.'

But Ryan knew it wasn't true. It hadn't been like that for the Outlier, and it wouldn't be like that for him.

He resented every punishment they gave him, every time they forced him to follow their stupid rules. He hated having to get up early to do stupidly long runs in the mud and rain. He hated having to write lines and clean corridors and shine his shoes. And he hated having to wear this muddy sports kit, day after day.

He wondered if one day, like the Outlier, he'd get revenge.

27. SENTENCE

The alarm beeped and Ryan rolled over and switched it off. He groaned as he rolled out of bed, then stumbled through to the tiny bathroom.

He looked at himself in the mirror, splashing water on his face and running a comb through his hair in a hopeless attempt to feel cleaner. Then he looked down at the filthy kit, double-checking the socks were pulled up high enough and he'd done up all the buttons on his rugby shirt. Today was not a day to make mistakes.

He picked up the folded piece of paper on the chest of drawers and headed out of the dorm. Ryan hoped that what he'd come up with was bad enough to satisfy both the sergeant and the colonel. Surely another five hundred lines and a month's worth of early morning runs would be enough? They couldn't expect any more from him than that?

As he approached the gym, he took a deep breath. Sergeant Wright and Colonel Keller were both waiting for him in the sports hall, a determined look on their faces.

Ryan marched in and saluted.

'Well, did you do as I asked?' demanded the sergeant.

'Yes, sir.' Ryan held up the piece of paper.

'This better be good, cadet. If you've done this properly, then you should be afraid of what's written here.'

'I am, sir.'

He wasn't, really. But it wouldn't be fun.

'I'll be the judge of that.' Colonel Keller snatched the paper from him. 'I bet this is nowhere near severe enough.'

Ryan didn't answer. He just stood there while the colonel unfolded the sheet and started to read. He realised now that he should have offered more. These guys wanted blood. There was no way the teachers would accept his suggestions.

To his surprise, the colonel smiled. 'Well, Jacobs. I have to admit, you have surpassed my expectations. I thought you'd suggest something pathetic, but this is pretty good.'

Is it?

Ryan was confused.

'Let me see.' Sergeant Wright took the paper and glanced at it. Then he looked at Ryan with interest. 'You think you deserve all of this?'

'Yes, sir.' It was a trick question. If he tried to back out now, they'd only make it worse.

'Well, I think this will keep you pretty busy for the rest of this term, don't you?'

'Yes, sir.'

Not really, thought Ryan. *Five hundred lines won't take that long.*

'The funny thing is,' said the sergeant. 'I'd have settled for half of this. But, as you've offered, let's see it through.'

'And that means, Jacobs,' added the colonel, 'that if you deviate from anything on this list or fail to follow through with all of your commitments, then every member of your dorm will join in. Do I make myself clear?'

'Yes, sir.'

That couldn't happen. Ever.

'And that will also happen if you complain about this, or try to wheedle your way out of it. The rest of this term is going to be hell for you, and the sooner you accept that, the better.'

Something was wrong here. An early morning run every day was bad, but it wasn't that bad. And he'd offered to run for a month, not the whole term.

Sergeant Wright handed the paper back to him. 'You might as well keep this. Study it hard. Make sure you don't forget anything.'

'Yes, sir.'

'Now, it's time for your run. Don't forget we'll be tracking you this time.'

Ryan scurried out of the gym and pulled on his trainers. Before he set off, he stood in the doorway and unfolded the piece of paper.

It took him a moment to take it in.

No, it couldn't be!

The list was totally different:

I will do a six-mile run each morning before drill and I will assist the canteen staff every lunch hour. Every day, after lessons, I'll clean the school toilets. At weekends, I'll clean all the boots in the boot room.

I'll also write 1,000 lines each week: "I am lazy, cheating scum and I deserve to be punished."

I will do all of this until the end of term and I won't complain.

How could it have happened? This wasn't what he'd written. It wasn't even his handwriting. Canteen duty and cleaning toilets every single day! A thousand lines every week!

And sorting out the boot room was a nightmare. At Devonmoor, students shared football boots from a school supply. They were stored in a huge, dirty room next to the changing area. There were a hundred or more pairs of battered, muddy boots in there, along with shin guards and other equipment.

'Something wrong, Jacobs?' Ryan looked up to see Sarrell standing behind him, smirking. 'The list not quite what you expected?'

'You did this?' Ryan's voice was strained.

'When I came to check on you last night, I saw your pathetic attempt at coming up with your own punishment, so instead of waking you, I thought I'd give you a hand.'

Ryan realised the full horror of the situation. 'I'm never gonna get any free time.'

Sarrell gave a wicked grin. 'That's right. Say goodbye to fun time in the common room. Say hello to cleaning a hundred pairs of football boots every weekend.'

Ryan opened his mouth to speak, then closed it again.

'Something you want to say, Jacobs? You look like you're going to cry. I told you I'd toughen you up.'

'It's fine. I can handle it.' Ryan didn't want to give Sarrell the satisfaction of seeing how upset he was.

'Good. Glad to hear it. Because I am going to be watching you. Every. Single. Day.'

This just gets worse and worse.

'Can I go for my run now?' He had to get away from Sarrell, before he said or did anything stupid.

'Of course, Jacobs. Have fun. I hope the wind isn't too cold this morning.' Sarrell laughed and walked off, as Ryan headed out into the darkness.

As he started across the field, anger burned inside him. It felt like Sarrell had won.

This round at least.

The term stretched ahead of him like a prison sentence. It had only just started. There were weeks and weeks of this, through the cold winter months. Every day would be hard. Every weekend would be grim.

But he'd get through, somehow.

And one day, Sarrell would pay.

***

His anger only got him so far.

Three days in, Ryan slumped on the floor, blinking back tears.

In front of him were racks and racks of football boots and shin guards. Next to him was a dirty sink with a cold tap.

While it was called the boot room, it was more of a cupboard. There was no daylight, and the room stank of sweat and mud. He could barely breathe. Cadets were meant to clean the boots after they used them, but most didn't do a great job, so now he had to pick up the slack.

So far, it had taken him all morning. He tried to tell himself the first weekend was the hardest: it would be much easier next Saturday. But he didn't know if that was true.

He had about another twenty pairs to do, and by then it would be time for his lunch duty—helping the canteen staff dish up the meals and wash up the pots. The worse part was that they made him wear a hair net while he scooped brown slop into the bowls. He was the laughing-stock of the academy.

And after that? He'd better make a start on the lines.

The door opened a crack and Lee slipped in. 'You ok, Ryan?'

Ryan sniffed and wiped his eyes with the back of his sleeve. He pushed himself up. 'Yeah. I'll be fine. I'm almost done.'

'Need some help?' Lee slipped off his jacket and hung it on the corner of the rack. 'Why don't I do the rest?'

Ryan was tempted. 'I dunno, Lee. If Sarrell or the colonel find out you helped, we'll both be for it. It's not worth the risk.'

'That doesn't sound like the Ryan Jacobs I know!' Lee joked and punched him on the arm. 'Come on, where's that rebellious attitude we all love so much?'

Ryan gave a weak smile. 'Fine. If you want to clean some, you go right ahead!'

'That's more like it.' Lee grabbed the wire brush with way too much enthusiasm, picked up the half-finished boots in the sink, and got to work. 'We're working on a plan, mate. We're gonna help you through this.'

'How?'

'These boots reek!' Lee held them at arms length as he worked. 'Sparks is building a kind of photocopier this weekend. He figures that if you write a thousand lines, we can copy them to use for future weeks.'

Ryan's eyes lit up. 'Will that work?'

'He thinks so. And he usually knows what he's talking about. And I'll chat to the guys about this as well.' Lee gestured to the racks of boots. 'If those of us who play at the weekend all clean a few pairs each, we'll soon have it done. Sarrell will never know we're all doing more than we should.'

'That would be amazing.' A glimmer of hope appeared in Ryan's eyes. 'Would you guys do that?'

'Of course. We can't help with the morning run, though. Or lunch duty.'

'Or the toilets,' said Ryan. 'Sarrell stands over me while I do those. It's his favourite form of entertainment.'

Lee gave him a serious look. 'You'll get through this, Ryan.'

Ryan realised Lee was right. He couldn't give in. He wouldn't live his life in constant fear. He wouldn't become a teacher's pet, even if he had to run for miles and clean toilets every day.

'Thanks Lee, I appreciate it,' said Ryan.

And he meant it.

Not for the first time, Ryan wondered how he'd ever survive Devonmoor if it wasn't for his friends.

28. SECRET

'Ryan, my boy! Did you get it sorted?' Mr Davids emerged from his office like a bear coming out of hibernation. Ryan realised he hadn't seen much of the teacher for days.

'I think so, sir. You were right. I shouldn't have given the robot, er, the program the chance to break the rules. I've fixed it now.'

'Good, good.' The teacher smiled and walked over to Ryan's computer. 'Goodness, my boy, is the colonel ever going to let you get changed?'

'Probably not. I wouldn't come too close. How about your project, sir? Did you sort out the program you were working on? The Chaos Flower?'

'What?' For a moment Mr Davids looked guilty, like a child caught stealing a chocolate bar. 'Oh yes, I've just finished. It works like a dream.'

'Glad to hear it.' Ryan yawned and logged off. 'I'm about done for the day. I'm heading off to the common room, unless you need me for anything?'

'No, my boy. You play with your friends. I'm quite happy down here with my machines.'

'If you're sure.' Ryan sometimes wondered if the teacher slept in his office.

He headed out of the lab. His muddy trainers sat outside the door. As he picked them up, something slid down inside. He stopped and looked. A memory stick. What was that doing in there? Who had put it there, and why?

Anyone could have done it. His shoes had been in the corridor for over an hour. There was no way of knowing who had walked past. People had been in and out of the lab all evening.

But if they wanted him to have this, why didn't they just pop in and give it to him? Why hadn't they spoken to him about it?

He peered through the glass door. Mr Davids had gone back into his office. The lab was empty. Ryan slipped back inside and made his way back to the machine in the corner.

This could be a trap, but as long as he didn't plug the stick straight into the academy network there was a limited amount of damage it could do. He pulled a cable out of the back of the computer, disconnecting it. Now it was just a standalone machine. If there was a virus on the stick, it wasn't going far. The network would be safe.

He stuck the memory stick in and opened the folder, wondering what was inside.

Just a video clip.

This looked less like a conspiracy and more like a student prank. Or maybe Sarrell was sending him a copy of the video of Ryan going crazy in a monkey cage, to remind him to toe the line.

Ryan stuck in some headphones, sat back and pressed play.

'Hello, Ryan.' The screen stayed black but the voice he heard was rich and smooth. He couldn't quite tell whether it was a man or a woman. 'I hear we have a lot in common.'

Ryan sat up straighter, suddenly alert. It couldn't be...

'My name is Sam, but you know me as the Outlier. They call me that at Devonmoor, as if it's a bad thing. But I was called much worse. I hear you have the same problem.'

Ryan wanted to reply, but he had to remember that this was a video, not a voice call. However good the Outlier was with computers, he wouldn't be able to hear anything Ryan said.

'I'm told that we're alike, Ryan. You are a rebel like me. You don't like following their stupid rules. And I imagine that means you get punished a lot.'

Too right, thought Ryan.

'I know how that feels. I went through it too. For years I had to wear that stupid uniform, pretending to be like the rest of them: the little obedient army cadets who follow any order they're given. But I'm different. And so are you.'

Was the Outlier trying to recruit him? Was he about to ask Ryan to betray the academy?

'They're using you, Ryan. Surely, you can see that? They're turning you into one of them. You don't even know it's happening. They make it sound so noble, so patriotic.' For a moment, the smooth voice became bitter. 'Save the country, they say. You can help save the world. Is that what you did this week, Ryan? When you stopped my little project in its tracks?'

Ryan felt hot. He wasn't sure what he thought.

'Thanks to you, I didn't get what I was after.'

The Fractal Processor.

'But I wasn't the only person who lost out. They probably told you I was stealing money. But I wasn't. I was simply redistributing it. That's why you'd never have found any way it made its way back to me. I'm like a modern-day Robin Hood. I take from the rich and I give to the poor. And few people are as rich as the Devonmoors and their little group of friends. People high up in the government, those who sit on the executive boards of large corporations, people who hold a lot of power. I broke their money down and I gave it to thousands of struggling families. They got to keep it, Ryan. Or they would have done, if you hadn't interfered. Mums who couldn't feed their children. Old people who couldn't heat their homes.'

Ryan shifted uncomfortably in his seat. He hadn't really thought about it until now. They never had found a way of tracing the money back to the Outlier. That much was true.

'It's not your fault, Ryan. They used you. Just like they used me. For years. To protect the status quo. To keep the rich in power. To prevent any change. And they'll keep doing it. You're their new pet. They'll make you do whatever they ask. I know you think you're immune, but they'll turn you into another little robot. They almost did it to me, one punishment at a time, one rule after another.'

He didn't want to admit it, but the Outlier was talking a lot of sense.

'Right now, you can't do much. I know that. You're stuck in that school with no way out. But one day it'll click. One day you'll need help, and you won't know where to turn. When that day comes, I'll be here for you. All you need to do is contact me at the web address I'll post at the end of this video. Use the contact form to submit a message, but start the message with the word "outlier" in capitals. That way, I'll get it immediately.'

The word 'OUTLIER' appeared in white letters on the black screen, as if to underline the point.

'I know you don't trust me. That's wise: you shouldn't trust anyone. But Devonmoor Academy is not your home. The sooner you realise that, the better. And next time, think twice before you interfere with any of my schemes.'

A web address appeared on the screen. It looked like it belonged to an IT company.

'That's the website you need, Ryan, if you're ever in trouble. Until then, stay strong, and don't let them break you. I look forward to meeting you at some point soon. Perhaps we can be of some use to one another.'

The video stopped.

He hadn't even seen the Outlier's face.

But he had heard what he had to say, and his head hurt.

Who were the good guys here, and who was bad? Was this all some cunning attempt to manipulate him into betraying the academy?

Or was this the truth?

He clicked on the link to see where it would take him, then realised the computer was still disconnected from the network. He plugged it in and tried again. It took him to the contact form on some dull company website: VORONMODE IT SOLUTIONS.

Not that he planned to use it.

Or did he?

His head hurt. He needed time to think. He logged off and headed to the common room.

This was no time to be choosing sides or making big decisions. Right now, he needed fun and friendship.

And a shower.

He really needed a shower.

EPILOGUE

'It's the last day of term. You must be pretty happy about that, Jacobs.'

'Yes, sir.'

Ryan stood to attention, alongside the other cadets. It was their final drill.

'Shall we see if you've learned your lesson?' Sergeant Wright asked. 'Show me your socks.'

Ryan lifted his trouser leg, revealing the long grey socks underneath.

'Well done, Jacobs! You managed to get dressed correctly yet again! It would have been a shame to extend your punishment into next term, wouldn't it?'

'Yes, sir.' Ryan would never have coped with that.

'You see, cadets,' said the sergeant, smugly, 'even little rebels like Jacobs here can learn to follow the rules. Will you ever risk wearing incorrect uniform again, Jacobs?'

'No, sir.'

'I think we're going to make a Devonmoor cadet out of you, after all.'

The sergeant strode off, continuing his inspection.

Ryan was relieved. He couldn't wait to get out of here and head home. He had two entire weeks of bliss to look forward to, and when he had to return to Devonmoor, it wouldn't be anywhere near as bad now he'd worked off his punishments.

After what felt like an age, they were dismissed.

Ryan filtered out with the others. As soon as they were in the corridor, they started chatting to one another about the plans they had when they got home.

'For a moment, I thought you might have done it,' said Lee, a sparkle in his eye.

'Done what?' asked Ryan.

'Worn yellow socks on the last day of term. Just to wind the sergeant up.' They'd joked about the possibility in the common room last night. 'But I'm guessing you decided it wasn't worth it.'

'Too right,' said Ryan. 'I couldn't cope with another term of torture.'

'Who would have thought they'd get you following the rules like a good little cadet,' teased Jael, listening in.

'Who indeed?' asked Ryan. 'But that doesn't mean I didn't take *any* risks.'

He glanced around to check no teachers were nearby, then lifted his trouser leg again. This time he took it higher, up to the knee. Above the grey socks was a yellow turnover from the football socks underneath.

Lee burst out laughing. 'You're such a legend!'

Jael shook his head in disbelief.

'I think I might always wear them like that from now on,' said Ryan, smiling. 'Just to remind myself I can still break the rules.'

And he meant it.

He had to keep taking risks.

He needed to prove that he wasn't some obedient cadet.

He was Ryan Jacobs.

And he wasn't afraid.

A NOTE FROM THE AUTHOR

Thanks for reading 'Code Zero'. If you're up for more of Ryan's adventures, check out the next book in the series: 'Shut Down'. In it, Ryan has to work out who he can really trust, before more innocent people die.

Maybe you'd also be interested in getting your hands on advanced copies of new books, before they even go on sale? If so then the readers' club is the place to start! Visit www.paulorton.net to join.

And could you do me a huge favour? I need you to review 'Code Zero'. Reviews on Amazon make a huge difference to a new author like me, and it would be amazing if you could write a sentence or two about what you liked about it. I'd really appreciate it and I promise I read every review.

Until next time,

Paul.

GET YOUR FREE E-BOOK

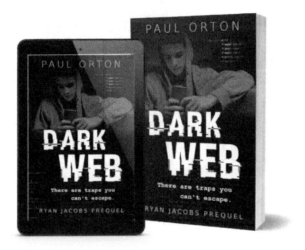

There are traps you can't escape.

When Ryan Jacobs asks to join the Faction he finds himself trapped in a situation which keeps getting worse. He needs to escape fast, or they will own him forever. But how can he fight an invisible enemy?

Find out about Ryan's life before he is taken to the Academy. DARK WEB is exclusively available to members of the Ryan Jacobs Alliance – sign up for free at www.paulorton.net

RYAN JACOBS BOOK 1

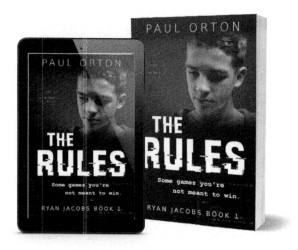

Somehow, he lost his freedom.

Now he belongs to the Academy, and the rules have changed. What started out as a game has become a matter of life and death.

If he doesn't think fast, someone will die.

At thirteen you shouldn't have to face these kinds of issues. But at thirteen, you don't get to decide the rules.

THE RULES is the first book in the Ryan Jacobs series and is <u>AVAILABLE NOW ON AMAZON</u>!

RYAN JACOBS BOOK 2

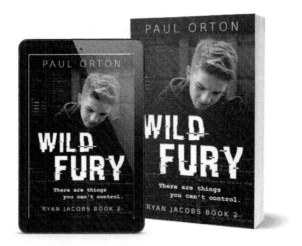

They call it the Fury. And no-one is safe.

Life has got very complicated for Ryan. The fact is that he's never been much of a team player. It's not easy when your friends hate you and everyone else is on your case. And that was before people started going crazy. He has to find some answers, and fast. Before things get out of hand. Before anyone gets killed. Or worse.

WILD FURY is the second book in the Ryan Jacobs series and is <u>AVAILABLE NOW ON AMAZON!</u>

RYAN JACOBS BOOK 4

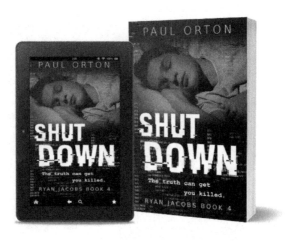

Everyone has secrets.
Even those you least expect.

Ryan is in trouble. He has to stop the shutdown but doesn't know who to trust. The authorities are closing in and he's running out of time. It's not easy being thirteen and having a reputation. Whatever he does, his enemies are one step ahead. But if he doesn't succeed, more innocent people will die. Will he uncover the truth? And will anyone believe him when he does, or will it just get him killed?

SHUT DOWN is the fourth book in the Ryan Jacobs series and is <u>AVAILABLE NOW ON AMAZON!</u>